ENID RICHEMONT started writing young. At eleven she was crowned Bard of a youth eisteddfod (a Welsh festival of literature and music). "At school," she says, "I could never make up my mind whether to be an artist or a writer when I grew up." In the end she did both.

After school she won a scholarship to Dublin College of Art and subsequently worked as a teacher in a community for children with mental disabilities. She then had a successful career writing short stories for magazines, before getting married and starting a family. As her children Jeremy and Polly grew up, Enid Richemont set up her own business, Cabbage Designs, marketing the toys that she'd made for them. It was to amuse her children that she turned once more to writing stories.

Her first novel, *The Time Tree*, was published by Walker Books in 1989 and she has since completed several more books, including two young adult novels, *The Game* and *My Mother's Daughter* as well as three stories for younger readers, *The Glass Bird*, *The Magic Skateboard* and *Kachunka!* She lives in London with her husband and two cats.

Books by the same author

The Glass Bird
Kachunka!
The Magic Skateboard
The Time Tree

For older readers

The Game
My Mother's Daughter

WOLFSONG

ENID RICHEMONT

WALKER BOOKS
LONDON

For Olivier and Marie-Christine

First published 1992 by Walker Books Ltd
87 Vauxhall Walk, London SE11 5HJ

Text © 1992 Enid Richemont
Cover illustration © 1992 Richard Parent

Printed and bound in Great Britain by
Richard Clay Ltd, Bungay, Suffolk

British Library Cataloguing in Publication Data
A catalogue record for this book is
available from the British Library.

ISBN 0-7445-2432-6

CHAPTER ONE

She's dead.

And he's being done for whatever the French call Drug Offences. Bet Martine's pleased. She never did like him.

I break off a finger of chocolate biscuit. Mum offered me those two pearls of information before we both left and I haven't had time to digest them yet.

Henriette. Dead.

I don't feel much; why should I? I only met her once. The coffee in the paper cup scalds my tongue. And him? I suppose you could say that was inevitable. So what? I look round the canteen for some light distraction, but all my friends are somewhere else.

I pick a guy at random. The shape of his head intrigues me, but the hair confuses things. He shifts slightly, revealing a smooth cheek line, no features visible — frustrating. I will him to turn and offer me more, but he doesn't respond. The same type? Could be. . .

I know it's just a game. I'm not looking for anyone – I don't need to now. But strangers do fascinate me; always have. People on the bus, people in the street – they're so virgin. I wonder about them, make things up. Must get that from my dad.

The snow glow from roofs and windowsills shows up brownish stains on the plastic table top and a feather of ash from someone's cigarette. I watch my screwed-up biscuit wrapper slowly expand against a curl of peel in the undersized ashtray.

Then I go back to the guy – well, there's nothing else to do. I grin – my eyes must be making little holes in the back of his head by now.

I think: supposing he turned round and there wasn't any face – just some smooth, featureless egg-thing?

Supposing he's fat and jowly?

What if he and I were the last ones left on earth so we *had* to do it?

What if he really turned out to be an Alain lookalike? I shiver . . . daren't answer that one.

It's OK, pretending. Doesn't hurt anyone. Steve does it all the time and he expects to get paid for it. Imagination, he calls it. Nurture it, he says. You were very imaginative when you were small, he tells me. I wouldn't remember.

So Henriette's dead. . .

I suppose they'll have her in that elitist graveyard? She must be acceptable now – they can't say *she* didn't die of natural causes.

I'm getting morbid again and I don't like it. I finish up the chocolate, roll myself a cigarette and return to the guessing game. What colour eyes? What kind of a mouth? Big blubbery lips? Thin cynical ones?

Boils? Acne?

What would he do if I walked round and checked? "Hi! I just came over to see what you look like from the front..." As if I'd dare.

That's the sort of thing my friend Amy would do.

I glance at my watch. I ought to be working. I stub out my cigarette and drop my cup in the bin, skirting cautiously round the Mystery Man, not looking, not cheating, not spoiling the game.

In the library I spread out my books. Racine. Molière. Whoever could care for Molière?

"Get your A-levels nicely tucked away," Mum always says. "Then you could take a year off before going to university..."

"Maybe she should take time off right now," argues Steve. "Get a job. Live a little. She'll come back to it all so much fresher..." Well, he has to cough up, doesn't he?

And having a fifteen-year-old daughter to support does spoil his image.

So here I am in this compromise called a Sixth Form College. Westgate Polytechnic. It's not school. So they tell me...

I pick up my pen. My mind drifts...

We go to Paris next April. On a coach. Paris in the spring. A whole luxurious week in a students' hostel – great stuff. I went to Paris from primary school and didn't think much of it then. Maybe this time it'll be different.

At least my French will have improved.

We went south once. To the hills behind Avignon. "*Sur le pont d'Avignon.*" Camping. When Hannah was little and Steve was still living with us (I called him Dad then).

No smoking, so I nibble the end of my pencil instead. Smoking's no big deal for me – just something to do with my hands at parties, something to keep me off the sweets and biscuits. It's cigarettes or spare tyres, that's what Amy says, and she ought to know. I do it sometimes at home to make Mum feel guilty: "Your influence," I tease her (she still smokes far too much for someone of her age). I never light up in Dad's place; Steve doesn't go for women who smoke.

The chill gold lattice of window patterns spills at odd angles across the spines of books. I see bits of sky between the office blocks all flushed with winter rose, and my heart sinks. It'll probably thaw tomorrow.

I scribble something irrelevant across the top of the page.

Chanson du loup. Chant du loup.

Well, it's French, isn't it?

I decorate the words with wolves' heads, big pointy teeth dripping gobs of blood. All the better to eat you with.

Chanson du loup. Song of the wolf.

Chanteloup...

No wolves left, Martine assured me, but I can

still remember how, at the beginning, I would lie awake, listening, scaring myself, half expecting some strange, melodic howling to come rising above all those nocturnal rustlings and flutterings. *Jungle Book* stuff... I was still a kid, back in the summer.

Amy turns up. She snaps her fingers in front of my eyes, making me jump. "Thinking great thoughts?"

I sigh. "Trying to write something intelligent..."

She spreads out her books and sits down opposite me.

"Henriette's dead," I tell her. "Martine rang Mum."

Amy shrugs. "Well it's hardly surprising, is it? She was pretty ancient..." She examines her nails. Her nails are long and pointed and she's coloured them alternately violet and emerald. She's roleplaying again.

I turn back to my Molière and, cribbing from footnotes, I fake up one or two brilliant observations.

Then I drift again...

The guy with the hair will be in some class or other. Maths? I grin: hairdressing? He'll never know that for a short time he was singled out by wonderful me. People know so little really, and when they guess, they get it wrong.

People make assumptions.

Look at Amy. Look at me.

We used to assume we'd be best friends for ever.

Well, we're still friends...

And look at Mum, always putting herself down...

But when the *Westgate Recorder* did that piece about her costumes, she came out all shiny and giggly. The effect of the flash, I suppose, but we hardly recognized her. And she's much tougher with Dad these days – really winds him up.

I return to my wolves.

Had there been life, I wonder, before Chanteloup?

CHAPTER
TWO

I didn't want to go there in the first place. We had other plans, Amy and I. Holland. Maybe Germany, Austria. Possibly France, but on our own terms. Hitching. We knew plenty of people who'd done it.

Then her lot screwed things up. No hitching, her dad said. Too risky; go on the train. But Ellie can't afford that, Amy'd argued. Too bad, he'd said. Then you'll have to do something else.

We were still trying to get it together when Mum dropped her bombshell.

"I'm taking Hannah to Brittany. Why don't you two come with us?"

My mouth dropped open. "We come into a fortune or something?"

Mum grinned.

"We're going to Martine's great aunt's place."

I worked that one out slowly, thinking about Mum's fat French friend.

"Martine is too old to have a great aunt,"

I said at last.

Mum squealed. "She's only a year older than me..."

"Exactly."

She let it go. Mum's really sensitive about her age. I suppose you get that way when you're past forty.

"It's a big old family house," she went on. "And they all have to do a stint at caretaking it – checking on the roof, airing the place, that sort of thing."

"Why doesn't her great aunty do it?"

"Because she's old and frail. Lives in a Home."

"So why ask you two?"

Mum lit another cigarette. "Company..."

"Well, she wouldn't want us as well."

"It was her suggestion," said Mum smugly.

"So what's wrong with old what's-his-name – Martine's bloke?"

"Charles?" Mum sighed out a curl of smoke. "Oh, he'll be on duty at the hospital. They're having their proper holiday later – Greece, I think. Charles says he's had enough of France after all these years. But Angus might come; he goes over quite a lot. Bilingual, did you realize?" She grinned. "Trust Martine to see to that! Got a whole bunch of friends over there – kids he met on family holidays, his age now... I thought you and Amy might like to hang around with them if they'll have you – do wonders for your French."

I winced. She does love organizing me and she does make such sweeping assumptions. I'd met

Martine's son only once and we didn't have much to say to each other then. He was into ancient buildings and weird music. A callow youth. I went for older men. As for Amy, she'd probably loathe him on sight.

And then there was Hannah.

I could hear my revolting little sister tootling away on her recorder in the next room.

"What's Hannah going to do there?"

Mum topped up our coffees.

"Well, there's a huge garden. Grand enough to be called a park, according to Martine, but neglected of course. And there are lots of little family beaches just a short drive away." She looked at me meaningfully. "You'd enjoy it."

I compared the horrors of a family holiday with our dream of hitching round Europe. I compared it with the possibility of youth hostelling in Hertfordshire. I measured it against the probability of taking a summer job in the cake shop down the road, and the cake shop definitely won.

But when I told Amy, she seemed quite interested.

"Why not?" she said. "It's abroad and it's cheap."

That afternoon she came back with me.

"You two could take the tent." Mum suggested idiotically. "Camp in the grounds. Be completely independent." Like kids, I thought scornfully. What a concession!

But: "Grounds?" said Amy. She was obviously impressed.

Mum pushed her advantage. "Oh, it's big," she

said. "The house is enormous. Get lost in it at first, Martine tells me."

"Sounds fantastic," breathed Amy.

Sounds like a nightmare, I thought, but who was I to argue? Amy'd always been the leader; I just plodded along. Even in primary school she seemed to be three steps ahead of everyone else. Once, when she was about ten, she slipped out and had her ears pierced, using some Christmas money she'd smuggled in. No one even spotted the gold sleepers under that bush of hair.

I was flattered when she seemed to like me. Reflected glory, I suppose...

I sigh and pick up my pen.

Amy reaches over and sweeps my pad sideways.

"You've written a lot..."

I groan. "Reams, yes."

"Chanteloup... Wish we were there now..." She frowns. "I like your werewolves..." Her breath smells of Fruit Gum. "You auditioning for the panto?'

I shake my head vigorously.

"Well, you ought to." She grins. "Follow in your mum's footsteps."

I think of my mum, belting it out twice a year in the chorus of the Westgate Operatic. I think of the flat, overflowing with gold braid and ribbon and market stall taffeta. "Don't be stupid," I say.

But Amy's already packing up. "Going to audition. Coming? Dare you..."

It's all very well for Amy – she absorbs facts

like blotting paper.

The sky has deepened to a shadowy crimson and the lights in the buildings opposite are a cold blue dazzle.

"I can't," I whisper. "Haven't done anything."

"You've written four lines," argues Amy, "if you don't count the doodles."

I watch her retreating, envying the coils of her hair, streaked copper with henna (it turns orange on mine). She's slimmed, but she's still too big for those leggings. The way she moves, it doesn't matter. If I didn't know her, what would I guess? Promiscuous? She likes to talk that way. Sexy? In spades. Intelligent? I sigh. Is my friend Amy bright? You should see her exam results.

I look blankly down at my text book.

Feet clatter on the stairs and voices echo in the hall below, but this place is sacrosanct – soft with whispers and the rustling of pages. It cocoons me.

I try to concentrate, but the sound of French inside my head makes me think of other things...

That cut-price crossing on the night ferry, for example, and Mum buying gin and tonics for herself and Martine.

"Don't we get any gin?" I'd grumbled, looking at the cans of shandy she'd brought us.

"It's age-ism," joked Amy.

"You mean reverse age-ism," corrected Angus.

Amy looked miffed. "Please yourself," she said stiffly.

I watched Martine settling down with her knitting. She's a super knitter; never uses a pattern. I watched her plump, satiny fingers moving effortlessly over the needles and tried to imagine those soft hands in white rubber gloves, manipulating a drill, bearing down on her victim with a hypodermic: "Open wide..."

Mum picks them! Whoever heard of a middle-aged, female dentist prancing about on a stage, squawking, "Three Little Maids from School"? Well, that's Westgate Operatic for you.

We went up on deck, Amy and I, with Hannah tagging on tediously behind. We stood, watching the drifting glitter of distant ships, the odd bobbing fairy light and the glow of our own monstrosity on the foam below.

"We rented a cottage once," Amy said. "In Connemara. Tiny job, with camp-beds stuffed into every room. Said it would sleep six – well that was a joke. Had to share with the kids. Not much fun."

"Will I have my own room in that house?" asked Hannah.

"Well, I'm not sharing with you."

"Oh, goody!" Then she yawned. "We nearly there?"

"No."

"Then what are all those lights?"

"Another ship, I should think."

We wandered up to the far end where there weren't so many people. The interior of the ship made me think of one of those out-of-town shopping centres, cheap and gaudy, with pinball

16

machines and a kids' cinema, but up there it felt real, with the wind blowing my breath away and a salty taste on my lips.

Hannah wrecked my fantasy of sailing through uncharted oceans. "I want to go down now," she whined. "Want to finish my book."

"I'll take you," says Amy.

I found out why Amy was so obliging when she returned with a couple of gin and tonics.

I gawped. "How did you get away with that?"

She grinned.

"No problem."

And I see us sailing into Roscoff through that silvery-grey sea mist...

The car deck smelled tarry and there was shouting and the clanking of chains – no soft music down there. We piled into Martine's big Volvo and waited silently. Well, not quite silently: I could hear my stomach bubbling. The coffee and toast Martine had insisted on was all mixed up with that gin and tonic. I don't usually tuck into coffee and toast at five in the morning. No wonder she's fat.

I considered Martine.

Martine was like an apricot, plump and edible, with fudge-coloured hair and freckled gold skin. Fat somehow suited her (it doesn't suit me). She made me think of one of those Oriental goddesses, all heavy and languorous – well she's got a bit of Arabic blood too, Mum says, so maybe that counts. A dentist? That was a joke. I sometimes wondered if she treated her victims to one of those arias while she was filling their teeth: "*Your tiny gum is frozen...*"

The minute we were through Customs we had to park the car and rush out to buy things. Hannah picked up an overpriced packet of sweets done up with curled ribbons ("just this once," warned Mum) and Amy and I drooled over the French edition of *ELLE*.

We squeezed back into the car. I tried to avoid too much body contact with Angus. He'd picked up some joky anarchist newspaper nobody but him could understand, and a music magazine, so he wasn't talking. He didn't talk much anyway. An arrogant bum, I was beginning to think. I did a flash analysis: an only child, spoilt rotten by his mummy. Not that he looked like his mummy, apart from the hair and those tawny lashes.

Which was just as well.

Fat blokes were something else.

CHAPTER THREE

I pack up my books. I never thought I'd do much.
Henriette has got under my skin.

Death. It's so final.

I catch the bus home, sitting zombie-like,
staring at street lights already swimming in slush.
Why do nice things like snow never last?

Hannah's had friends back. They're squatting in
a huddle on the sofa, watching a video. When I
come in, they start whispering, giggling. I suspect
they're laughing at me.

I ignore them and help Mum with supper. "I'm
going to bed early," I say. I ought to call Angus
but I can't.

"You OK? You haven't eaten much."

"I'm fine." I look meaningfully over at the kids.
"Just need a bit of peace and quiet. Got to get
some work done."

Hannah comes to bed at about half past nine.
I can hear her mattress creaking as she wriggles
around.

"Ellie?" she calls plaintively. She wants to natter.

I fake sleep. With the lights on it's not easy. Mum's put up a curtain between our two beds – gold-spangled sari stuff she found in a market – but I still long for my own space, a solid door to shut between myself and the world.

I remember my room at Chanteloup. My room? Alain's room. But perhaps some ghost of me still hovers over that puff of a bed, or lies between the folds of those thin linen sheets I was so scared of ripping.

It's not just dead people who have ghosts.

Hannah snaps off the light. I open my eyes. I can hear Mum running herself a bath and I grin – she'll start singing soon; she's convinced we can't hear her. Leading roles, of course. The parts Martine usually gets.

Then I relax and let my thoughts slide backwards. . .

We stopped at St Nazaire for our first taste of Breton food – buckwheat pancakes stuffed with bacon and cheese, and little bowls of cider. Amy'd done her eyes and put on some lipstick, but her hair was wild.

"Can't I have some cider?" grumbled Hannah.

"No," I snapped. "You're too little." I felt mean. I was hot and grubby and I was sure I smelt bad.

Then Angus made a point of calling the waitress and jabbering away in French. Show-off, I thought. The girl went all smily. Then she came back with a glass on a tray. She set the glass in front of Hannah.

"*Mademoiselle*," she chirped.

Hannah looked suspicious.

"Try it," said Angus.

Hannah took one sip and her face became ecstatic.

"What is it?"

"*Sirop de Grenadine.*"

"Oh, wow!" she said. "Oh, yummy! I'm going to have this all the time."

"Not at that price," said Mum.

By the end of the meal Hannah was already making goo-goo eyes at Angus, and inside the Volvo, perched on the luggage like a leprechaun, she rested her pink forearms on the back of his seat and began chatting him up.

Amy nudged me and rolled up her eyes.

I said, "Oh, shut up, Hannah. Do."

"Why should she?" said Mum defensively, through her usual haze of smoke. Well, Hannah's Mum's baby.

We crossed the toll bridge over the Loire and followed the road for what seemed like ages.

Suddenly Martine turned into the parking lot of a scrubby-looking supermarket. "We'd better stock up," she said, "or there'll be no supper."

We unhitched a couple of trolleys and went inside. Straight away Hannah dragged me off to look at satchels and pencil cases and to try on espadrilles that didn't fit.

We caught up with Amy and Angus in Books and Records. Angus was frowning over some psychedelic rock album while Amy browsed sweetly through a paperback on wild flowers.

"Didn't think your French was up to that sort of thing," I sniped, but she fluttered her eyelashes at me.

"I'm looking at the pictures, aren't I?"

After we'd loaded the car we turned our backs on the low shimmer of the sea and moved inland. Then we entered a maze of little lanes – English meadows and hedges simmering under a hot blue sky. It could have been Cornwall. It could have been Wales...

I suddenly remembered the name of the house. Chanteloup. We'd already translated it, of course. Something to do with a song, we supposed. And something to do with a wolf.

"Are there really wolves?" I asked naively. "And do they really sing?"

"You sound like Hannah," teased Mum.

When Martine had worked out just what I was asking, she laughed. "No wolves left, Ellie."

We turned into a courtyard. A black Labrador came out of a barn and began bounding round us, wagging its tail and barking madly. Martine pulled up and opened the door.

"Hey, Jules!" she called. "*Viens, Jules!*" The dog put its front paws into her lap and tried to lick her face. She ducked and pointed. "There's your wolf, Ellie."

An elderly couple came out of the cottage, a slow, heavy old man with a mauvish complexion and a picture-book granny in a wraparound apron.

"*Bonjour*," called Martine and she and Angus

climbed out to greet them, hugging and kissing them while Jules leapt about excitedly, trying to join in. Then Martine waved back at us. "*Mes amis anglais*," she announced.

I suddenly felt ridiculously alien, as if I'd turned green or grown another head. I'd always known Martine was French, but it had never meant much – she was just Mum's bouncy friend with the funny accent. As for Angus, with his French mum and his Scottish dad, I'd just labelled him English. The old alliance, Mum jokes about his parents, but when I ask – what's that? – she tells me: read your history books. Does she ever stop being a teacher?

It had felt so different when I came over with my school class, or when we'd gone on holiday, ages ago, with Dad. We were in a group. All the same. All speaking English. I mean, *they* were the foreigners then.

Martine came back waving a bunch of keys that could have come straight from the set of one of the Westgate's old operas.

"They wanted us to come in for drinks," she said, restarting the engine. "But if we'd done that we'd have been there for the rest of the day. And Monsieur Auguste would have insisted on helping and he's got a dicky heart."

"Who are they?"

"Caretakers. Been there ever since I can remember. Be retiring soon though; a nice comfortable little apartment in Nantes, with fitted carpets and central heating – that's what they need at their age."

23

Amy was staring at the empty stables. "Are there horses?"

"Only wolves." In the mirror I could see Martine winking at me. "There's an ancient donkey, I remember – if she's still around. Old Margot. You can ride her if she'll let you."

We rounded the corner and scrunched slowly under a canopy of ancient oaks that bordered a sunlit lawn. And then I saw it.

I shall never forget my first glimpse of Chanteloup – its square tower, its steep copper-green roof, its biscuity walls warmed by the dying sun and its window eyes lidded with white wooden shutters.

Amy gasped.

Hannah squealed, "It's like a palace!"

Martine laughed. "You won't say that when you see the inside." She pulled up on the gravel. "I will unlock," she said, rattling the keys. "Then comes the hard work."

We followed her out, Angus with that slightly hippie jacket crumpled at the back, and Amy holding out her T-shirtful of crisp crumbs like a kid with an old-fashioned apron.

Mum was stamping about and flexing her legs. "Well?" she said, looking smug. "Glad you came, you two?"

"You bet," said Amy, but I said nothing.

Hannah began jumping around. "It's super, super, super!" Her voice went all squeaky.

I stood, blinking into that olive-gold evening, my body still vibrating with the rhythm of the car.

Mum started unpacking. "Come on, you lot."

Amy flicked her fingers in front of my face. "Come back, Ellie."

Angus had dumped one of the food boxes and was standing, gazing at the house.

"This place is older than it looks, you know," he said. "That nineteenth-century facade is built round something much earlier. Seventeenth, isn't it?" he asked Martine.

Show-off, I thought, but Amy was clearly impressed.

"D'you mean century?" she enquired dumbly.

And Angus sighed. "What else?'

We brought all our bits and pieces into that dim cavern of a kitchen, then hung about, suddenly shy, watching Martine and Angus being at home, opening shutters, then windows, checking on cupboards, turning on the electricity. Even Mum didn't quite know where to put herself. It was their family's house. It was their country.

Martine caught me staring at the formidable row of heavy copper pans hanging against the wall.

"You like cooking, Ellie?"

I shrugged. "So-so."

"Well, if you want to use that lot, you'll have to cope with dust and spiders and goodness knows what else." She waved at a heavy oval dish with two handles. "They found a hornets' nest inside that one, someone told me."

"What's a hornet?" asked Hannah.

Martine spread her hands. "A big wasp." Her voice lowered. "Who knows? It may be still in there." Hannah faked terror and hid behind Mum. Martine pointed out a big enamel casserole and a few ordinary-looking pans, quite bent and battered. "We usually use this lot." She picked up some cans of beer and popped them open. "Glasses in the cupboard, Chrissie," she said to Mum. She poured out orange juice for Hannah. Then she held up her tumbler of golden liquor.

"Cheers," she said. "And welcome."

CHAPTER
FOUR

When we'd knocked back our drinks, Martine yoked herself between two cases. "Come on, you lot," she said. "Let's open the place and get settled in."

Mum objected. "I'll take mine; you can't carry both."

"Yes, I can," said Martine.

Mum rushed forward to help.

"Go away," said Martine. "I'm nicely balanced. Look."

Mum sagged, defeated; then she toddled out after her. Next to Martine she looked small and meek and I found myself feeling protective. I like Martine but I wouldn't want her as a mum. There's just too much of her, in every sense of the word.

We followed them into a big shadowy hall. Angus switched on a wooden candelabra, which gave a flat yellowish light. "You can play ping pong here," he said. "The gear's in that cupboard."

He went on up the stairs and we came after, Amy stooped under her graffitied duffle-bag and Hannah clutching her ancient bear and her satchelful of junk.

Martine unlocked the linen cupboard.

"*La lingerie*," she announced. "The real stuff, too. None of your cotton polyester here. And old. God knows how old."

Mum asked, "Who does the washing?" Well, she would.

Martine smiled.

"The Augustes. There used to be a *blanchisseuse* – a washerwoman. Then the Augustes got themselves a machine. Now Monsieur picks up the stuff from the house and Madame irons it."

"We can't let her do that for us," protested Mum.

Martine shrugged. "She's proud of her ironing. Try stopping her."

Angus had disappeared up another flight of stairs. We could hear him pounding about, like the ghost in the attic, somewhere above our heads.

Martine said, "You must start choosing your rooms. Angus always has the same one – he goes straight to it. Like a cat, you know? I've reserved the big one at the end of the corridor for your mum and myself." She grinned. "We get first choice, because we are the oldest. Also it has two beds. You go now. Explore. Then give me a call and I'll show you how to deal with the shutters."

It was like a kid's party game – opening doors,

switching on lights, squabbling over treasures.

"I want this one..."

"Well, so do I..."

"Well, I found it first..."

"This one," shouted Hannah from afar. "This one's mine. Aymee! Ellie! Come and see my room!"

She switched off the light to surprise us.

I remember a dark bed shape in one corner, and the sun needling through cracks in the shutters, tinselling an old cane sofa and making little amber snail trails through bunched folds of curtain.

Hannah switched on the lamp and then I could see that the curtain was lace, that there were buttercups on the bedspread and faded pink stripes on the wallpaper, and that against the window wall stood a leather-hooded dolls' pram and a small wooden cradle.

"Oh, pretty," sighed Amy.

We called for Martine to show us how to open the shutters and the lamplight paled inside a wedge of warm sun. Hannah started bouncing on the spindly sofa, sending little puffs of gold dust into the air.

"This is my room," she sang.

"I can see that," said Martine.

"So you all go away now."

"OK, OK. We know when we're not wanted." Martine laughed. "Plenty more rooms."

"I want a room with a double bed," said Amy dreamily.

"Oh, yes. What are you planning?" I teased.

"Oh, not what you think. Anyway I wouldn't

want to share it. I've never slept in a really big bed; I'd want it all to myself."

My own room, I was thinking. Mine. I haven't had a room to myself since Dad left and we had to move into the flat.

Amy charged up the second flight of stairs. "Come on up!" she yelled, as if the place belonged to her.

I was suddenly embarrassed. It didn't feel right. It wasn't even Martine's house, and there we were, galloping all over it as if we owned the place. I wanted to see the next floor too, but I followed Amy with reluctance, walking primly in the opposite direction as soon as we got to the top. Through a half-open door I caught sight of Angus pottering around in his room, and already I felt like an intruder. I scuttled past, too self-conscious suddenly to explore any further.

That was how I found it.

It was inside the tower and I walked dumbly into it. My room. I switched on the light – hessian-shaded and smelling of dust – and saw two painted silk fans on a peppermint green table, a puff of dried hydrangeas in a pewter pot, and beyond those, long thread-bare curtains, knotted and twisted, with feathery slits in their water-stained lining. I crossed the room, pulled open the window, unlatched the shutters and stepped back into a rectangle of brilliance which gilded the floor-boards and turned a threadbare rug into a magic carpet...

My room.

It had been waiting for me.

There was the bed, large but not quite double and covered with that thick duvet-thing, and against the end wall a massive wardrobe (much too grand) with mouldings and garlands, glowing russet under a bloom of fine dust. Over the bed there was a portrait – a romantic, black and white photograph of some young man, slightly misted at the edges and mounted inside a big oval frame. Adjacent to it, on a small shelf, stood one of those crimson candle burners you sometimes see in churches. I grinned. So what was he? A saint?

I found a little alcove with a clothes rail just wide enough for one or two dresses. There were a few things still hanging there – a threadbare maroon jacket, a belt, a couple of ties and a funny-looking shirt. The space below was stuffed with boxes and papers and old magazines, yellowed and brittle.

But straight away I began riffling through them, looking for the flat wooden box – I seemed to know it would be there. I opened it boldly, parting layers of oiled paper to uncover a whole spectrum of unused pastels. My fingers itched to try them out, but that wouldn't have been fair. They belonged to someone, didn't they? Anyway, I can't draw.

I closed the box reluctantly and put it away. From somewhere else I could hear Amy calling, "Ellie! Come and see!"

I heard her opening doors along the corridor – "Ellie? Ellie?"

Then she was standing in the middle of my

room, an intruder, touching, interfering, judging things.

"Pongs a bit, doesn't it?" She fooled about with the fans, investigated the alcove, peered at an ancient print of Nantes, bounced on the bed, considered the portrait: "Quite sexy if you like that sort of thing." Then she tugged at my arm. "Come on. Come and see where I am."

"Not now," I said quickly.

"Why not?" grumbled Amy. "I came to see your room."

"I've got to unpack."

"Well, so have I. So has everybody."

I unzipped my small suitcase and began pointedly taking out my stuff and piling it up on the rug.

Amy looked baffled. "What's the matter?" she asked. "What have I said? What have I done?"

"Nothing. Honestly." I made an effort. "I just want to do this first. I'll come in a sec."

"OK," she said, miffed. "But you'd better..."

I returned to my alibi and, reluctant to invade that grand wardrobe, pushed back the things on the rail to make room for my shorts and my jeans and my one fancy skirt.

Then I sat on the bed, inside that big soft hollow Amy'd made in the duvet, and wriggled round to examine the portrait. I could see what she'd meant – that old-fashioned film star face, the eyes deep-set and hypnotic, the lips fine but sensuous and above them the fairest hint of a moustache – well, wow! But those early photos can make anyone look romantic. He was probably quite boring. Some grocer. Some lawyer.

I prised myself free from those unprofitable musings (he was either dead or geriatric, so no use to me) and went to sort out my bedding with Martine; that duvet seemed much too bulky for summer.

I could hear her long before I found her, down in the kitchen, tipping salt into a pan of hot water and belting out some crap about a gypsy prince. Mum was sitting at the table, her eyes all swimmy, chopping onions and knocking back the *vino*.

"There's no mattress in my room," I said. "Just some weird duvet-thing."

Martine chuckled. "Then that's the mattress. No duvet-things in this house."

"That thing?"

"Feather. You try it. It's good." She put a lid on the saucepan. "Ravioli for supper. Which room did you choose?"

"One on the top floor. At the far end. The one that goes into the tower."

Her face went all funny.

"That's Alain's room."

I was shocked. It had felt like mine.

"You didn't say there was anyone else . . ."

"There isn't."

"Then who's Alain?"

She ignored me. "A bit tatty, isn't it? There are much nicer rooms."

"I like it," I said defensively.

"I thought you two would want to share," said Mum.

Oh God, I thought.

"Those ragged old curtains," Martine went on. "And I believe it's quite damp."

Was she was trying to put me off?

I called her bluff. "Would you prefer me to sleep somewhere else?"

"Not at all." She laughed. "I said choose and you've chosen."

So I went back upstairs and took out sheets, pillowcases and a fawn blanket with green stripes. The sheets and pillowcases had knife-edge creases and smelt of blancmange. I handled them warily. Linen, I thought. They were old – I could see that. And some of the little darns had missed and that worried me – what if I caught my toenails in the gaps?

I made my bed reverently, drawing the soft, bobbly blanket over that sharp criss-cross of folds, and tucking everything in. No little sister on the other side of the curtain, I gloated. This was my space.

There was a chair, like something from one of those Van Gogh paintings, with a woven straw seat and a bleached wooden frame. I dragged it over to the open window and sat looking out at that unreal landscape, the golden lawn where swifts were flying low, dipping and darting into the long shadows, the dark pointed reeds that suggested a pond, the big old chestnut trees and the mysterious woodland that thinned to a pale meadow.

Somewhere in the house a bell began to ring, strident, bossy, a clang-clang straight from a primary school playground, and Martine's voice came carolling up two flights of stairs.

"Supper."

It shocked me out of my reverie. Obediently I went down. I wasn't really hungry.

Amy had brushed out her hair and put on a mauve sweatshirt with turquoise zigzags. She looked up at me.

"Where've you been all this time?"

"Making the bed," I said vaguely. "And un-packing."

"My God," said Amy. "What have you brought? Full evening dress?"

Mum ladled out the ravioli while Martine tossed a salad.

"You eat an awful lot of lettuce," grumbled Hannah.

"Good for you," said Angus.

"Can't stand the stuff myself," said Amy. "Then I'm a junk food addict. Hamburgers, baked beans and loads of chips – that's me."

"Plenty of those things around here," sighed Martine. "Even our little resorts are beginning to sprout their own home-grown Macdonalds. France is changing."

"It has to," said Angus. "Our lot aren't quite as obsessed with their stomachs, for one thing. Can you imagine Gaëlle spending half a day over her *pâté feuilletée*?"

"Her patty what?" asked Amy, to annoy.

"Flaky pastry to you," said Martine. "And as for Gaëlle, she could buy it frozen from any super-market."

"Who's Gaëlle?" asked Amy sharply.

Angus shrugged. "An old friend..."

Hannah was passing out over her pot of yoghurt.

"Bedtime," said Martine. "For everybody, I think." She began scraping plates into a big dustbin. "A long day, *n'est-ce pas*? We will wash up in the morning."

When I switched on the light in my room a large grey moth fluttered in and settled over the brown hessian shade. Almost immediately, another one brushed past my hair and began flying round my head.

I screamed and Angus came running. It would have to be him.

"What happened?"

"Moths," I said, flapping about and feeling foolish. "I'm dead scared of them."

"And you leave your shutters wide open?" He laughed. "There are bats out there too." He drew in the shutters, leaving a gap. Then he caught my tormentor, scooping it delicately into the cup of his hands, and released it into the night.

He trapped the other one inside a tumbler, sliding a card under the rim.

"You want to see?"

I backed off.

"Look – it's beautiful. Won't hurt you."

But I didn't want to know.

He tipped it out and fastened the shutters.

"No more moths." He grinned at me. "*Bonsoir*," he said. "*Bonne nuit*." Suddenly he seemed much more French than English. Their country, I thought.

His country.

Mum and Hannah, Amy and me – we were foreigners. That was a funny feeling.

"Thanks," I said vaguely. "See you tomorrow."

CHAPTER
FIVE

When I turned off the lamp, I felt as if someone had glued up my eyes. The darkness was absolute, no concessions, no vague edges to things, no silhouettes, no dim familiar shapes, no shapes, no up, no down, no sideways. It was like a box. There was no window. There was no door. I panicked and reached for the switch.

I can't sleep with the light on, so I got up and paddled around. I borrowed some magazines from the pile in the alcove, but my French wasn't up to it. I felt cross. I was tired, I wanted to sleep, but if I switched off the lamp, it was like being blindfold. I'd never been afraid of the dark before, but then I'd never seen that much dark. I curled up on the bed and tried to nestle between two of those funny square pillows but it didn't work.

I even began listening for the singing wolf, but all I picked up was a tweeting bird. Then I started to drift. Alain's room − so who was this guy

Alain? Did he come here often? Were those his clothes on the rail? I twisted my head and looked up at that portrait. The shadowy eyes seemed to focus on me. I stared right back. Could this be their Alain? The sexy saint?

I must have slept eventually, because when I opened my eyes again the lamp seemed paler and there were flecks of plum coloured light across the wardrobe. I looked at my watch. It was almost ten. I found that hard to believe. I got out of bed and opened the shutters and found that the day had been around for hours, that the sky was an established blue and that the sun was already fingering the shadows on the lawn.

When I stepped tentatively outside, the whole place felt like a fairy castle – frangible, unreal. It smelt funny too – musty, foreign. I went downstairs, curling my toes round the middle of each step where the wood had been worn to a dip. Sunlight ringed the banisters with gleams of mahogany, but across the powdery-green walls of the bathroom on the next floor there were streaks of dried bird crap.

Down in the kitchen I found Mum and Amy and Martine sitting glumly over big bowls of coffee and tea.

Martine looked up at me. "Sleep well?"

"Not really," I said. "It was too dark."

"You English," teased Martine. She pointed at Amy. "Your friend had the same problem."

"Moths," I said. "Hundreds, and I'm terrified of them. Angus had to come in and close the shutters."

Amy yawned. "He fixed mine too. Heard you screaming and flapping about – thought you'd broken a leg or something."

Mum spotted my embarrassment.

"I wonder how Angus found out *you* were scared of moths, Amy?" she asked sharply. Oh, she's cunning, my mother. But then you can't work with kids for as long as she has without picking up some form of self-defence.

Amy quickly changed the subject. "You could have opened those shutters a crack, you know. After you'd put the light out. That's what I did."

Martine poured me a milky coffee. "Tomorrow we'll get ourselves croissants," she said. "Can't have a proper French breakfast without croissants."

"Where's Hannah?" I asked.

"Still asleep," said Mum. "I think yesterday was a bit much for her."

Amy said airily, "Angus always sleeps late."

"How do you know?'

"Martine told me."

We relapsed into an uneasy silence. Then Martine got up and went over to the sink. "Come on you two." She threw us a couple of tea towels. "I'll wash. You dry. And we'll leave your mum in peace to enjoy her first cigarette."

As usual my heart sank as I watched Mum light up. She'd gone into serious smoking soon after Dad left and it was getting worse. I'd started to roll a couple of my own – Amy'd shown me how – but that was peanuts; Mum just couldn't afford it. Then there was that thing about lung cancer. What if she died and there was no one but Steve? Dad was OK but he'd got his own life – his job, his bloody Muse and those workshops he ran on his *Philosophical Fables*, published by that fringe outfit which had long since gone bust. Not to mention his current girlfriend.

Penny. She was only a few years older than me.

I thought: Why aren't women like that? Why can't Mum have a Muse? Why doesn't Mum lust after some schoolboy?

"Mum," I said. "D'you ever fancy a toy boy?"

Mum looked startled. "Got someone in mind?"

"*The flowers that bloom in the spring, tra-la,*" trilled Martine.

"*They'd have to take under their wings, tra-la,*" Mum sang back. "*A most unattractive old thing, tra-la . . .*"

"Stop putting yourself down," I said. "You're not that bad. Considering your age."

There was a knock.

Martine shouted, "*Entre!*"

M. Auguste unlatched the back door. He hesitated, looming against the light, awkward and shy, cradling something against his blue dungarees. Then he stepped timidly across the flagstones and laid four green hand grenades on the kitchen table.

"*Pour vos invités.*" He treated us to a toothy grin.

I could see Martine looking secretly at Mum. "*Oh, vous êtes trop gentil, Auguste.*"

He shrugged, his arms against that thick body

suddenly limp, purposeless. *"Oh, c'est normal."* He looked at Mum and proudly tried out his few words of English. "You like, madame?'

Mum nodded enthusiastically. "Very much."

M. Auguste gathered himself together. *"Bon. Je m'en vais."*

"Those things look dangerous," said Amy.

"Artichokes." Martine smiled. "He grows them."

"My God, why?"

"They're nice to eat," said Martine. "I'll show you."

Incongruously a telephone began ringing – a sharp single note repeated over and over again. Martine rushed out but returned almost immediately. "It's for Angus." She sighed. "It begins."

"What begins?" asked Amy.

"He has many *copains* – friends – down here. Some he has known since we first started coming, but some are new. You will meet them perhaps." Mum smirked knowingly.

"I thought Angus was asleep," I said.

"Oh, but he is," said Martine. "Standing up. By the phone. You should see him – a sleep-talker." She began tidying things away. "Shall we go to a beach today? Picnic?"

"Sounds good to me," said Mum. "I'll go and rouse up Hannah."

Amy nudged me. "Come and see my room," she said. "You still haven't, you know."

I went upstairs to please her.

"Wait." Amy loves high drama. *"Durum. Durum. Durum . . ."* She did a fake roll of drums as she opened the door. "What do you think?"

I took my time. I could play the critic too, walking about, peering at things – the little mirror with the plaster cherubs (two fingers and a nose missing), the crackly portrait of a sour-looking parson – all black, with white collar flaps; a print of some ancient captain who went down with his ship, and that elaborate "family" tree with the heads of all the popes done in little oval frames. I prodded the balding green velvet of a gilded chair, poked at the long linen pillow-sausage on the unmade bed and admired the ragged swirls of patchwork that covered the sheets.

"Not bad," I conceded. "This bed's big enough for three."

Amy bounced on it, grinning. "I'm planning an orgy . . ."

"Prefer my room," I said at last. "I've got Mr Sexy, haven't I?"

I sat down next to her. The mattress was like a rock. "I've got a feather bed," I crowed.

"I know. What's it like to sleep on?"

Not much good last night, I thought, but I wasn't letting on. "Odd," I said. I considered. "You sort of lie in a hollow and it heaves up round you."

"Sounds like being seasick." Amy got up. "Listen. You ain't seen nothing yet. Come and look at this." She walked over to the wardrobe and opened it.

I gasped. The inside was stuffed with clothes – furry things, silky things, feathery things handbags, shoes. I picked up a beaded evening bag.

"Who do they all belong to?"

"Everyone, I suppose," said Amy expansively. "Every woman who's ever lived in this house."

"That would be a lot." I remembered Angus's remark about nineteenth-century whatnots built on to seventeenth-century thingummies.

Amy eased out a dress – a swathe of ivory silk with a sprinkle of seed pearls. "What about this one?"

"Put it back," I said nervously.

"But it's Thirties. Look." Ever since she'd had that part in the school pageant, Amy'd considered herself an expert on costume. She held the dress against her and spread it out and I saw that it was cut in floaty panels, with a deep vee outlined in sequins and little pearls.

When I picked up the fabric it rippled through my fingers. "It's beautiful," I whispered.

"Put it on."

"Don't be stupid. It belongs to someone."

"Whoever it belonged to has long since snuffed it."

"Perhaps it belongs to Martine's great-aunt."

"So what? It wouldn't fit her now. She'd be ancient."

"That's a bit mean," I said.

"But truthful."

I said, "You put it on."

"Wouldn't fit me," said Amy. "It needs someone skinny like you."

"I'm not skinny," I said. "Look at my hips. . ."

"Not as big as mine," said Amy. "Anyway, you've got small bones. Go on. Dare you."

"Shouldn't we be getting ready for the picnic?"

"Getting ready?" mimicked Amy. "So what are you wearing – a cocktail dress?"

"Oh, shut up."

I took off my shorts and my T-shirt. Then I lifted the dress and let it fall over my head, over my body.

"Wow!" said Amy.

I stepped back, trying to put some perspective, some distance, between myself and the image in the mirror. The shining girl trapped behind the cold glass moved with me, and when she moved, sequins glinted like sundrops in a stream. Somewhere in the house someone turned on a radio – piano music, jazzy stuff, not my kind of thing, but I found myself moving to it, swinging, turning, hypnotized by the patterns of silk curling and swirling...

"Look at you," giggled Amy.

So I looked.

The dress was amazing, but the face was all wrong. Well, it was my face. It would be.

I tried changing it, plonking a plummy Cupid's bow over my pale lips, and pink blusher on my cheeks, and pencilling my eyes in black so they looked enormous. I even got rid of my long droopy hair and gave myself a stylish haircut, a little straight fringe. It was very convincing.

Too convincing.

I stuck out my tongue, but the girl in the mirror just went on smiling. I blinked, but she didn't blink back.

I panicked. "Amy," I yelled. "Come and look in the mirror..."

"How can I when you're hogging it?"

I pointed. "That's not my face."

Amy scrambled over the bed and put her chin on my shoulder. "Looks like Eleanor Portman to me, honey child."

I pushed my nose up against the glass and saw my own mousy lashes and the spot that had started yesterday. Imagination, I thought ruefully. Wish I could get paid for mine.

"Shall we call Martine?" said Amy. "Or Angus? Show you off?"

"They'd be livid."

"Know something?" said Amy. "I think he fancies you."

"Angus? Help me off with this thing. You must be joking." Some kind of enchantment fell away with the silk.

"You looked amazing," said Amy. "You ought to make more of yourself. I'm always telling you that."

I sighed. "There's too much of me as it is."

"Let me do your eyes."

I grinned.

"For a picnic?"

CHAPTER
SIX

The kitchen reeked of Martine.

Bouncing about in a cloud of duty-free scent, she was fussing over the cold box Mum was packing. As soon as she saw us she said, "We must leave at once," as if we all had to flee from some disaster.

"Why?" demanded Hannah.

"Because we'll miss the *boulangeries*." She pulled a face at Hannah. "Bread shops to you, miss."

"No, we won't," yawned Hannah. "They won't go away."

"Ah, but here," said Martine as we followed her out, "they close at twelve. On the dot!" And she locked up the house with those pantomime keys.

The Volvo, devoid of its cases and boxes, seemed suddenly cavernous. I sat, hemmed in by Amy and Hannah, all straight and narrow, keeping myself to myself, not wanting to dilute that sexy sensation of silk against skin.

"Where's Angus?" asked Amy.

"Oh, he's not coming. Going out later with friends..."

I looked back and watched the house retreating behind the dappled drifts of green and gold. I wanted to stay. A beach was just a beach. Sand, sea and sun – the same anywhere.

Martine hooted as we drove past the Auguste's cottage; then we re-entered that maze of lanes. We followed the road sign to St Michel-Chef-Chef. The name gave Hannah the giggles. "It sounds just like a train – listen. Chef-chef; chef-chef..."

"It meant something ecclesiastical, I believe," said Martine, "but I can't remember what."

We parked under the trees in the square. She'd been dead right about the *boulangeries*. Two of them looked as if they'd been closed for years, but the woman locking up the third one turned and recognized Martine.

"*Madame 'amilton, quelle bonne surprise!*" She smiled at us. "*Vacances?*"

We nodded and grinned like a row of puppets.

"*Mes amis anglais*," declared Martine.

"Ah," said the woman, as if that explained everything.

"*Et vous cherchez du pain.*" She opened the door and we went inside. She sighed heavily as she arranged four *baguettes* in a row on the counter. "*Et la pauvre tante?*"

Concentrating hard, I managed to pick up one or two predictable comments on the awfulness of old age. Not bad, I thought. But I'd have learned a lot more if I'd been on my own with Amy.

Martine handed us the loaves. "Two each."

"I want to carry one," insisted Hannah, so I handed her mine.

We went back to the car and drove down to the beach, leaving the Volvo under the shade of a squat little palm – at least that was exotic. Then we trailed in a crocodile, wading heavily through the warm sand, meandering round the parasol tribes, with Hannah and me trying not to gawp at the display of boobs (I never knew the female breast came in so many shapes and sizes). I suddenly found myself missing Angus, not for himself, but just for his maleness. Five women, I thought. Me and Mum and my best friend and Mum's best friend and my itsy bitsy sister. Yuk.

Mum noticed my silence.

"Penny for them," she said irritatingly. No deal, I thought. They were my thoughts, not hers.

We established our camp, spreading out the beach towels and arranging the goodies. A naked toddler paused in his concentrated waddle to stare at us – well, I could see why. Mrs Hamilton was setting herself up for the sun. The Madras shorts had already been slipped off to reveal a russet and gold bikini bottom. Then she took off her shirt and undid her bra.

Someone called out, "*Viens, mon chéri! Viens manger, petit!* " and our tiny Peeping Tom took himself off.

We tucked into our feast. The pâté got peppered with grains of sand, and salad dressing dribbled over Amy's chin. Martine bit into the crackling half-cup of a *baguette* and crumbs scattered over her breasts like golden rain. Hannah went very pink and I tried not to stare too hard at that deep cleft and those mauvish-brown nipples. Had she fed Angus out of those things? The thought was embarrassing.

Then she lolled on her side like one of those Venuses in paintings. "You lot are over-dressed," she declared, anointing herself with sun lotion.

Never one to turn down a challenge, Amy straight away rolled the top of her one-piece swimsuit until it sat like a belt around her hips. I'd seen her naked before – in the shower at the swimming pool, but now she looked, somehow, different. Provocative.

Hannah came over and sat on my stomach.

"Go on," she said. "Dare you."

Even Mum was displaying her negligible goodies. "Go on Ellie," she encouraged. "It's all right."

"I know," I snapped. "You don't have to tell me."

Hannah pulled off her cotton dress and began prancing about in her Marks and Spencers knickers.

"It's OK for some," I grumbled.

"I want to swim," said Hannah.

"You must wait until the picnic goes down," said Martine.

"Oh, why?"

"Because," snapped Amy. She stretched out on her back. "Go on, Ellie. Don't be a wimp."

I had just committed myself when a group of people paused in their trek across the endless dunes.

"*Salut!*"

When I saw one of them was Angus, I rolled on to my stomach and began playing with the sand, patting it flat and doodling little patterns with the tip of my sunglasses.

I could hear them going through the usual routine.

"*Salut, mon fils.*" That was Martine. "*Salut, Gilles; salut, Michel; ça va, Gaëlle? Annick?*" I waited for it and it came. "*Mes amis anglais . . .*"

I looked sideways, eyeing that collection of bare toes raking the sand.

"You said St Brévin," grumbled Angus.

"So? I changed my mind," said Martine. "St Michel's not so far."

I could hear Hannah prancing about. She was already picking up the lingo. "Saloo," she was yelling. "Saloo, saloo!"

I turned modestly, propping myself up on one elbow.

Gilles was grinning at Hannah. "*Salut, petite!*" He turned to Angus. "*Anglaise aussi?*"

"*Mais oui.*"

"*Alors!* She speak better English than me." He pulled a face. "At her age . . . not fair." His feet, from my angle, seemed enormous, his toes monumental, his toenails like ringed shells. Above slate-coloured jeans he wore an embroidered waistcoat and a Celtic-looking medallion in some kind of dull metal. Not bad, I thought, in a hippie sort of way – gaunt and poetic, with straggling dark hair – but I did wonder bitchily if the guitar case strapped across one shoulder was just part of the act.

Angus introduced us all. "*Madame Portman*," he said, like a caller at a pantomime ball, "*et sa fille Ellie et son amie Amy.*"

The spiky blonde pushed up her oversize sunglasses and flashed us a wide, toothy smile. "We go," she said, struggling, "to the bar. You wish to come?"

"Too hot to move," I said, flopping over my knees and watching an ant struggling with a flake of crust. "Thanks all the same."

Angus looked at Amy. "*Et toi?*"

"*Moi?*" teased Amy, slowly curling the top of her swimsuit over her enviable, rosy-brown breasts. "Can't. No money. *Mon argent est dans la maison.*" Her accent was atrocious but she didn't give a damn.

The girl with braided brown hair and silver hoop earrings shook her head and laughed. "No problem. We pay. It's not much. You pay another day – OK?"

Mum frantically waved a couple of notes at me. "Go on Ellie. . ." and I knew I was letting the side down, not acting like her idea of a teenager.

I smiled apologetically. "Sorry – *je suis fatiguée.*"

"You OK?" asked Mum as they all wandered off.

I sighed. "Why shouldn't I be?"

"Can I swim *now*?" pestered Hannah.

"Oh come on," I said, resigned.

When we got back, I stretched out on the damp towel, letting the sun blot up the wet from my swimsuit. Hannah flopped with a book; fooling about in the water had used up even her excess energy. Mum was flat out in a sun-worshipping trance, and Martine, her peachy tan protected by an open shirt, was peacefully knitting.

My eyelids warm, I half dozed, slipping back again into that fantasy of silk, silk brushing against my skin, silk stockings sliding over my bare legs, silky panels fluttering like wings from my shoulders, silk flowing like cool water over my breasts, my hips. . . I half opened my eyes and for a while lay there, watching the small hypnotic movements of Martine's body as she knitted.

The question slipped out of me: "Who's Alain?"

Martine gave a little jump.

"Ellie," she said. "I thought you were asleep."

"You said I've got his room."

She shrugged.

"They've always called that room Alain's room. Because of that old photograph, as much as anything. He'd be – let me see . . . that's right – he'd be my great uncle. If he'd lived that long."

"He's dead then."

She'd begun knitting again, the needles tip-tapping. "In his early twenties, yes." She didn't look up. "One of those family tragedies."

"What happened?" I asked eagerly. I have this depraved taste for gruesome details.

"Stop probing," said Mum. She had just woken up. "Why, why, why. . . It's none of your business, now is it?"

Martine smiled.

"It's not important. Ancient history. Don't snap at her, Chrissie." She turned back to me. "He drowned."

That sounded quite shocking, after my romp with my little sister in those friendly waves.

I stopped probing, to please Mum, and promptly changed the subject to something much worse.

"That wardrobe in Amy's room is full of the most amazing stuff," I blurted.

"Oh, all of them are," said Martine calmly. "The house is like a history book. You should look inside yours."

"Can I?" I asked clumsily.

"Of course. Just remember – you are my friend's daughter and I trust you."

That shocked me. "Listen – I wouldn't dream . . ."

"Well, there are those who would," said Martine shortly. "Nice, respectable friends of my family too." She sighed. "If anyone ever draws up an inventory, some of those things could be worth a small fortune. But look at them, do. Please. Feel free."

"Well, thanks," I said, already feeling guilty.

Later Amy returned alone, running, breathless and snappy, her bare toes sending up little fountains of sand.

"You should have come," she said to me. "They're a great crowd. You'd like them."

"Well, maybe I will," I said vaguely. "Next time . . ."

"You know, I'd rather stay round here," I confided to Amy when we got back to the house.

"There's so much to see and we haven't even started."

"The grounds, for one thing," Amy agreed. "All we've really seen is the lawn."

So after supper we decided to explore.

"Go with them," Martine said to Angus. "Give them a guided tour. Show them the bush house and the lake and see if Margot's back in the meadow."

"They can find those things for themselves," said Angus, who'd just set up a game of Solitaire. "They don't need me."

"You're right. We don't," agreed Amy rudely.

"Can I come?" whined Hannah.

"You can come with me if you like," said Angus. "In the morning."

"Oooh, yes please."

"She's got a real crush on him, hasn't she?" Amy said as we walked across the grass.

I nodded. "She'd trade me in for a brother any day."

We paused to look at the slightly stagnant pond in the hollow of the lawn, while the swifts swooped about us like jet-propelled butterflies. Then we ducked under the fence and went wandering across the meadow.

"I love that PRIVATE sign," I said when we reached the barred gate that opened on to the road.

"Me too," said Amy. "Listen – I'm an elitist. I mean, if I owned a place like this, I'd put up signs all over: AMY NOLAN'S HOUSE KEEP OUT." She sighed. "People like Martine are so lucky."

"Well it isn't really Martine's either."

We followed the hedge, then turned, walking into our own stretched-out shadows. The wilting grass burned under the evening sun.

Amy slipped her arm through mine. "Let me tell you about Angus's crowd," she said. "They're really interesting. Into folklore in a big way. That guy Gilles is a vocalist too; performs at local gigs. He's a kind of nationalist as well. I mean Brittany isn't France, you know."

"Suppose not," I agreed vaguely. Folklore? I couldn't see Angus dancing round a maypole. His taste seemed to run either to the classics or to bizarre French rock bands. "Is Angus into that stuff?"

Amy laughed.

"Not really, no. I mean, not the type, is he? Anyway he's English – why should he care?"

"Half French," I reminded her. "And the other half's Scottish and that's Celtic."

Amy shrugged. "*Tant pis*," she said, with disconcerting expertise.

We entered the woodland on a rabbit path that dipped and vanished. A halo of small insects moved around our heads and dried leaves scuttered under our feet. Out of a distant tree a bird rose noisily, making us jump, and somewhere a dog began to howl. I thought about wolves, and shivered.

The lake displayed itself suddenly – a sheet of dark-veined gold with a small island nestling at its core. Under dipping willows a boat lay tethered, a black wedge against brilliance.

"Wow!" breathed Amy. "Shall we take it out?"

"I'm cold," I said. "Let's go back to the house."

"But it's still warm." She turned to me. "You're scared," she said. "What's the matter?"

"Nothing."

She slipped an arm round my shoulder. "You're a wimp, Ellie Portman; that's what you are. You ought to take some risks, you know, or you'll never grow."

"Have you grown?" I asked sharply.

"I'm growing. Look." And she stripped off her shirt and began capering about, bouncing her boobs like a stripper. Challenged, I joined her, prancing and giggling until the chill disappeared.

"We could swim at midnight," yelled Amy. "We could take out the boat..."

"We should ask Martine first," I said primly.

"Oh God, Ellie," groaned Amy.

CHAPTER SEVEN

I was jolted out of a deep slumber by Hannah jumping on my bed. "Come and see what I've found." It still felt like the middle of the night.

Through slitted lids I gave her a withering glance. "Go away."

"But I've found a secret room – don't you want to see?"

"I'm asleep."

"No you're not," she said, "or you wouldn't be talking."

"I'm not talking," I snapped, and I pulled the blanket up over my head.

"Meanie, meanie," she chanted.

When she'd gone away, I came up for air. I'd wedged open the shutters and slept so well. It was pleasant to lie in a room mapped out by moonlight instead of in that scary black box of the night before. I'd even stayed awake for a while, just for the pleasure of it, listening to the unfamiliar sounds of a traffic-free night and scaring myself by imagining wolf calls.

For a while I lay, looking at the soft slant of sun diamonds across the wall. Then I slipped out of bed, wandered foggily over to the window and sat, gazing down through a garnet triangle of Virginia creeper. That brat, I now realized, had hauled me out of the middle of a dream. I spread the shutters wide and breathed in the cool blue of the sky and the flat copper-green of the lawn. A crazy kind of a dream; it was still clogging my mind. I'd been dancing like a maniac to some old-fashioned music played on a lousy hi-fi, my little pointed shoes moving in and out of a flurry of silk. I grinned: wishful thinking – I had the wrong size feet for shoes like that. . .

Downstairs in the kitchen Hannah was playing at being everyone's pet.

"You should see what your sister found," said Amy accusingly. "A little secret room."

Martine looked smug. "I knew it was there, but I didn't breathe a word."

"It's got a four poster bed for dolls!" screeched Hannah. "And a dolls' sofa and this yummy little chest of drawers."

"Great," I said, pouring milky coffee into a blue and yellow bowl labelled NATHALIE. "Who's Nathalie?"

"I have another surprise," said Martine, ignoring my question, and she whipped out an ancient straw hat covered with little rainbow ribbon rosettes, which she plonked on Hannah's head.

"Ooh!" said Hannah, preening herself disgustingly. (I can't stand my little sister when she's being twee.)

Then Martine and Mum made things even more sickly, catching Hannah's hands and chorusing: *"Three little maids who all unwary, come from a ladies' seminary..."* and the little horror joined in with all the right words.

Angus walked into the middle of this ghastly spectacle with yet another perk: "Want to explore the garden?"

Hannah looked like she'd woken up to two Christmas stockings and her voice went all husky. "Yes, please."

"You are a meanie," goaded Amy after they'd left. "She told us you wouldn't come."

"Well I was *asleep*," I snapped irritably and stomped out.

In the back garden, along one of the narrow tracks between rows of vegetables, M. Auguste, peaceably fussing over his leeks and artichokes, seemed a lot saner than any of my lot.

"Bonjour," he intoned heavily, leaning on his hoe. *"Fait beau."* And he stroked the sweat from his nose. "Jollee weather," he added proudly, and looked really pleased when I nodded and smiled. At least someone thought I was OK.

I followed the track to the end of the vegetable garden and into a strip of neglected woodland that marked the edge of the estate. The sun, moving over that side of the house, had just begun to probe the cool brown shade of the thicket, picking out a dry leaf, a grass stem, a flower, and splashing paint-box emerald over small patches of moss.

I felt close to tears. Did all families have this effect on people, or was it just mine? I suppose in a way I was jealous – I wanted to be everyone's sweetie-pie too. It's so easy for little kids to be adorable. Put me in a straw bonnet with roses and I'd look like a donkey.

I stumbled on a kids' den made out of bushes. They'd done a good job – the branches interwoven with string and coloured rags, the curve of the entrance almost perfect. Inside I found two small, weather-bleached chairs, a candle end on a "table" made from the top of a barrel, a few screwed up sweet wrappers and a grimy bottle of cobwebs.

Intrigued, I flicked an ant off one of the chairs and sat, squeezing my fifteen-year-old bum between the wooden rails. I looked round admiringly at the leafy dome – better than any den I'd ever made. I began to think about the kids who'd constructed it. Angus's cousins? Maybe even Martine, at some time in the past. That made me laugh. I could just see Martine, plump and bossy, with an orange pony tail and a frilly frock...

Then I fell into fantasizing about all the children who might once have played there, fooling myself into picking out echoes of their voices – "*Ici... Viens ici...*" – among the chirpings of the birds above my head. Perhaps Alain? I caught myself quickly; I was getting obsessed.

But it wasn't hard to imagine that sensuous

face transmuted back into childhood. I could see him: Alain with no moustache, his unruly fair hair damp-combed flat by *Maman*. And later, in that drab uniform he loathed... I began making the place nice for him (would he have homework this weekend?), rearranging the furniture, carefully brushing the earth and dead leaves from the table top. I even found a stone to chalk out our secret game. Come and play with me, I pleaded. Don't say you're too busy again...

I heard a twig snap. I saw the leaves shaking.

"Alain," I whispered.

A small, grubby face peered at me curiously. Then it withdrew.

"*Y'a quelqu'un là,*" some infant shrieked.

Then Hannah poked her face inside. She was still wearing that hat and she looked ridiculous. "What are you doing in Catreen's house?"

"It's not Catreen's house."

"Well, it's not yours either." She turned to the younger child. "My grown-up sister," she said scornfully, pointing at me, and the kid, taking her cue from Hannah, covered her mouth with her hand and giggled.

I got up. "Have it," I yelled at them. "Go on. Take it. I couldn't care less about your baby games!"

I ran back through the vegetable garden. The house was full of light, the big double doors at the front were wide open and they were all out on the terrace – Martine, Mum, Amy, Angus and a couple of people I hadn't seen before. I blinked as I entered their brilliant sunshine.

Martine smiled at me. "Hello, Ellie. Want a drink?" She mixed me some pink stuff.

"What's that?"

"It's kir. *Gros Plant* – that's our local wine – mixed with blackcurrant."

We went through the usual pantomime – handshake, *bonjour, bonjour*. "This is Marie-Luce, M. Auguste's granddaughter. Hannah's out playing with her little girl."

Mum grinned at Angus. "Took her neatly off your hands."

"Oh, she was no trouble," said Angus. "I like kids."

"And this is Guy, who teaches English at the *Lycée*."

I shook hands with him too – the gesture was becoming almost automatic. Guy must have been about fifty, I guessed, and he ponged of aftershave.

I watched him with my mother.

"So you are the dress designer?"

Mum laughed and went pink. "I do the costumes for the local Operatic Society. Not quite the same thing."

"It's the same talent." He offered her a cigarette.

"I really shouldn't," she simpered, taking one. "Bad example for Ellie." (As if that were the first time I'd seen her smoking!)

"Wonderful stuff, English comic opera," said Guy. Comic opera? Well, Mum had had to do something comic to get Steve out of her system. "And those librettos – crazy!"

"You've been to Gilbert and Sullivan, then?"

Martine laughed. "Guy was a student in London."

"I'm always planning to give one of those librettos to my students," said Guy. "Pinafore, perhaps."

Mum looked astonished. "You know *Pinafore*?"

"Of course. The university put on a performance. I sang." He suddenly looked bashful. "In the chorus, naturally."

"Good God," said Martine. "You never told me that."

"I do not tell you everything."

An old flame, I suspected. Watch it, Charlie, I thought. He'd be the right sort of age, too. Well, wicked old Martine.

But it wasn't Martine he was flirting with.

Perhaps I'd better warn her. After all, what did Mum know about men? For the last five years her world had been nothing but kids' projects, New Maths and the local Operatic. One or two blokes, perhaps, but when they'd seen us they'd just faded away.

Guy was talking to Angus.

"You have grown," he observed. People do, I thought drily. "You will go to university soon?"

Angus reached for an olive. "Not necessarily . . ."

"Architecture," explained Martine. "Not many places; not many jobs. Charles was hoping he'd go for medicine."

"I may not," said Angus, "*go* for anything, *Maman chérie*. I might just bum around."

Guy nodded gravely. "In London or Paris?"

Marie-Luce was sitting with her hands folded shyly over her neat cotton skirt, turning polite grey eyes on each speaker and not understanding a word. I knew just how she felt.

I tried to help. "*Votre petite fille,*" I said bravely. "*Elle a quel âge?*"

She came to life immediately. "*Cathérine? Elle a six ans.*"

I desperately worked out some kind of response.

"*Bon,*" I said woodenly. "*Bon...*"

Martine came to my rescue.

"It's noon," she said. "Lunchtime."

Amy shook her head. "Does lunchtime always happen at noon?"

"It's the law," said Angus solemnly. "In France they guillotine people who eat lunch at the wrong time."

"Oh, Angus," said Martine. She turned to the others. "You'll stay of course? *Tout simple – on piquenique à table –* "

"*Oh, je ne voudrais pas,*" murmured Guy politely, but his body language was saying: yes, please.

"*Vous êtes trop gentille, Madame 'amilton,*" said Marie-Luce demurely. She sat up very straight. "*Mais où sont les gosses?*" and an unexpectedly powerful voice transformed her completely. "*Cathérine!*" she yelled. "*Viens ici! On mange!*" So much for my character assessment.

"Oh, my God," said Martine. "Look at this!"

A moth-eaten donkey led by M. Auguste was slowly making its way across the lawn.

"Look at me!" squealed Hannah, clasping

Cathérine round the tummy.

"Poor Margot!" said Angus. "You're much too heavy..."

"No, we're not," said Hannah, her feet almost brushing the grass.

M. Auguste lifted each of them off with a: "*Voilà!*"

"*Vous mangez avec nous?*" Martine said.

"*Oh merci, madame... J'ai du travail.*"

"Angus," said Martine. "Bring out the table."

"Need some help?" offered Amy.

"He doesn't," said Martine, "but I do. Come on."

It was an odd lunch, I remember. We set up an assortment of chairs around a big trestle table. Then Martine illogically spread a white cloth and handed round checked napkins rolled up in silver rings. We went in and out of the house like cuckoo-clock people, with plates of salami and ham and tomato salad and little pots of gherkins and mustard and a bowl of fruit and bottles of wine and water. "*Bon appétit*," said Martine.

I watched Cathérine and Hannah communicating in their own strange cocktail of English, French and sign language. I saw Marie-Luce deep in some incomprehensible discussion with Martine. I watched Guy chatting up both Mum and Hannah, and felt Amy withdrawing from me to engage in one of her complex battles with Angus. I concentrated on removing the little transparent rings from my slices of salami. Then I took a large apple and left and no one seemed to notice.

I wandered round the house – Martine had told us we could. I perched on the chair with the dangling springs and ran my fingers over the sprays of leaves delicately carved on its arms. I went into the dining-room (we will eat there on Sunday, said Martine) and sat in one of the high-backed leather chairs with the big brass studs, looking at the silver and porcelain in the glass-fronted cabinet.

In the adjacent room I found a statue of a bishop, his crozier tipped with ivory and his eyes, beard and robes stained in places with colour (how old was he? I wondered). I went into the library and looked along all the gold-lettered spines – Dante's *Inferno* and *Histoire de France* and even my old friend Molière. Then I squatted irreverently on the moth-laced yellow velvet of an ancient sofa and wondered if he'd sat there once.

Alain . . .

Could you fall in love with a photograph?

Upstairs, I went back to that face which now seemed to dominate my unmade bed. Down in the garden I could hear Amy calling me: "Ellie! Where are you?" Why should she care? I thought. A butterfly came fluttering through my wide-open window. "Ellie!" That was Mum. I looked down and saw the table being dismantled, saw the little procession moving across the lawn with plates and glasses and watched Martine raise the cloth against the sun like a big white sail.

I moved away and the brittle hydrangeas scuttered against my arm. I thought of all those ghost children around the bush house, their high voices chirping above the trees, and of me chalking up a game I didn't know how to play.

What was time? I wondered. Was it circular, like someone once said? Might you get yourself on to some kind of carousel and go back and change things? Make sure Dad's book never got published? Make Penny's family emigrate to Australia? Stop Alain from drowning?

But now he'd be ancient. As old as Henriette.

So what was time?

Alain's paper eyes looked into mine and time dissolved. I could feel him calling me: Ellie, Ellie...

"Ellie!"

I whipped round and saw Amy standing square in the doorway, her face framed by that heavy mane of hair.

"Where the hell have you been?"

"Around," I said vaguely.

"We're going over to Pornic. Want to come?"

CHAPTER
EIGHT

That afternoon went badly.

A sea mist had moved inland, shrouding the sky with a thin sulphurous haze. Outside the supermarket at Pornic Martine fanned herself with her handbag. "I'll be glad to get into the cool," she said. She smelt of cologne, but I could see the dark patches under the sleeves of her jacket.

"I'm too hot," whined Hannah. Strands of her fine, beige-blonde hair were sticking to her cheeks.

"So is everyone else," snapped Mum. Her eye make-up was melting and her grey-threaded curls lay flat against her scalp, making her head seem small and mean. As if to prove it, she turned on us. "You two will have to start mucking in a bit more," she grumped. "We're not going to shop *and* cook, day in, day out!"

"That's not fair," I said. "You just haven't asked us."

"You shouldn't wait to be asked. You should know."

I exploded. "Do you think we're psychic or something?"

"What's bugging you?" asked Amy as we took ourselves off. "You've been in a black mood ever since lunch."

I said nothing.

We tried on sandals and played about with samples of cheap cosmetics, trying them out on the backs of our hands.

"I was the invisible woman, wasn't I?" I admitted at last. "And I didn't like it."

"How come, invisible?" Amy sloshed on some glittery green stuff, then wiped it off.

"Nobody talked to me." I heard myself and I sounded like a kid. "I even went away and nobody noticed."

"So who were we calling then? Father Christmas?"

"Anyway I couldn't stand that creep making up to my mother."

"Guy? Oh, Ellie! He's an old friend of Martine's."

"Wish he was her lover boy."

"Well, maybe he is. We don't know, do we? Oh, Ellie, your imagination." It was OK for Amy. Her two had this conventional, old-fashioned marriage; they even looked alike.

Even the beach was a let-down − grey, damp and horrid. Disliking each other, we went back to the house, but the battles went on until long after supper.

One of Angus's friends dropped in − a solid-looking guy with pale blue eyes and one of those

Asterix moustaches.

Angus looked embarrassed. "I'm off then," he said.

"Oh?" said Martine. She held out her hand. "*Salut, Edouard.*"

"Party," mumbled Angus, avoiding our eyes. "Over at Michel's. Forgot to tell you." So that was why he'd changed, I thought. Amy'd already commented on the African print shirt.

"*Et la politesse?*" said Martine sharply, glancing pointedly at Amy and me.

Angus rubbed the back of his neck. "Don't wait up."

"I never do," said Martine.

"Can I come?" pleaded Hannah.

"Not this time," said Angus.

For one awful moment I thought Amy was going to let the side down and say: What about us? but she stayed cool. Turning to me she said, "Let's try out the ping-pong."

"Yes, please," said Hannah.

"We'll set it up for you," said Angus, too eagerly.

"*Mais – elles peuvent venir,*" muttered Edouard.

Amy picked that one up. "We don't particularly want to," she looked at me, "do we?"

Hannah skipped in and out of the hall, getting in everyone's way. "Bags the first game!"

"Oh, Hannah," said Mum. "Leave the girls alone, do."

"We have much better games in the library," said Martine tactfully. "You help me clear the table and we'll go and find them."

We heard Edouard's jeep grinding against gravel, then moving off. I glanced enviously across at that tight little trio – Martine, Mum and Hannah. I needed to talk to Mum. I needed to say it. "You weren't taken in by that Froggie creep, were you? I mean, you've got us, lovely us. Anyway, he's too old."

Martine was running water into the big stone sink. "Guy's a sweetie," she said, as if she'd been reading my thoughts. "We've known each other since we were kids."

"Does he have any children?" I asked obliquely.

Martine laughed. "What a funny question. None that I've ever heard of. His marriage ended years ago. Likes the company of women but nothing ever seems to come of it. Very easy to have around, though – good at saying nice things to people."

Oh, an expert, I thought cynically.

"Old-fashioned courtesy," drooled Mum. "We could do with a bit more of that."

"Coming, Ellie?" said Amy, and I followed her out. "Challenge!" she dared me, slashing viciously at the ball.

She served.

I provoked her. "Why were you so miffed?"

She drove the ball back at me. "So were you."

I sent it flying over her head. "You fancy Angus!"

She missed. I served.

"The trouble with you, Ellie," Amy puffed, her face all scarlet and her hair all freaky, "you've got these heavy sexual fantasies!" and she slammed the ball against my chest. "Why don't you just screw someone and get it out of your system?"

Have you, then? Have you? I wondered. After all, Amy'd always been first...

I lost that round.

That was the night there was a bee in my room. I never saw it but I knew it was there, skulking behind the wooden roses on top of the wardrobe, zizzling in the dark, getting ready to launch an attack. I fastened the shutters in a vee, keeping the bats out, but everything else in. Something small, nasty and triangular had already settled over the street map of Nantes, three lacewings were doing a suicide ballet round the light bulb, while the invisible enemy went on biding its time, furtively buzzing. It would have been too childish to call for Mum; anyway she'd be with Martine. Angus could have fixed it, I thought. He'd fixed the moths.

I twisted my head and looked up at Alain. So you fix it, I joked. But from his pale oval, Alain gazed back, his dark eyes impassive.

I crossed my fingers, put out the light and the zizzling stopped. So Alain *had* fixed it. I grinned – that was crazy. I listened. Nothing. Was it coming to get me?

I forced myself to think about something else. Why don't you just screw someone? Amy'd said. Well, had Amy? She had a constant queue of male hangers-on, but I guessed that she hadn't. Her parents were too strict for one thing. The checks they'd made before letting her come to

France with us, you'd have thought a fat lady dentist and a primary school teacher were running some kind of white slave trade.

I closed my eyes and found Alain's face inside my head. I sighed – men were different then. If he'd fancied me, he'd have come come asking Dad for my hand: "Mr Portman, although I am unworthy to touch the hem of your daughter's dress..."

I tried translating that into French: "Monsieur Portman..." I was still working on it when I felt his warm breath on my cheek, and when I put out my hand I could follow the contours of his face on the pillow.

Beloved, I thought...

"*Ils sont tous partis*," he whispered.

"Oh no," I said. "Only Angus. The others are still around..."

His cheek was smooth against mine, his satin-sleek hair slicked across my skin. "*C'est impossible*," he whispered. Well, I thought so too, but it was happening.

I put out my fingers and traced the curve of his lips below the unexpected roughness of the moustache. He must have kissed me, I know he kissed me, because his tongue tasted of cinnamon and tobacco, but when his hand slipped under my pyjama top, I began to shiver; what had happened to that old-fashioned restraint? No, I said, we mustn't; but his body was already crushing me. I began to panic – could you get AIDS from a ghost? I pushed him away and jerked myself awake, jumping, falling and not falling.

Weeping. I loved him. I hadn't wanted to say no...

I sat upright and gaped at my other-world image in the wardrobe mirror. I moved and the girl in the crumpled nightgown shifted too, then meekly buttoned her pyjama top at the same time as me. I blinked; that dream had confused me...

It was then that I heard it.

"There *are* wolves," I said accusingly to Martine the next morning. "I heard one last night."

"Oh, Ellie," said Mum. "It was probably some farm dog."

The atmosphere was tense. It was nearly eleven and Angus still hadn't come home.

"I found these little printing blocks. Look," said Hannah. She had that daft hat on again and the tip of her tongue was stained blue.

I dutifully admired a repeat pattern of blue and white cows. "Brilliant!"

"I think we'll go and look at windmills today," said Martine brightly. "There's a working flour mill – ever seen one?"

"What about Angus?" said Amy.

"Oh, he'll turn up."

Mum lit a cigarette. There were already three stubs in the ashtray; I'd counted them.

"You'll get lung cancer," I joked as usual, but I didn't find it funny. I poured myself a coffee and sat staring at the grey silhouettes of twigs and leaves on the sunlit dust of the windows. What if she did get cancer? What if she died?

Amy was at the sink, peeling hard-boiled eggs. She glowered at me. "You might give us a hand."

"I've got a headache," I lied. "Do you mind if I don't come?"

"Oh, don't say that," said Martine. "I'll get you some aspirin."

"I'd really rather stay, if you don't mind." Excursions were never my scene, even when I was ten.

Mum looked embarrassed. "You'll feel better out in the fresh air, love. You can't stay here by yourself."

"She can if she wants to," said Martine. "The Augustes are around."

"Oh, come on Ellie," said Amy, "or I'll be stuck with Hannah. Not that I mind of course," she added quickly, seeing the expression on Mum's face (you can't say things like that about Mum's baby).

"What's the matter?" Amy asked me when we were alone.

"Nothing much. Just didn't feel like it."

"I don't either. I'll stay with you if you like."

I composed my reply very carefully. "I was actually going to have a go at some of those books. You know, work at my French."

"Ellie," said Amy slowly. "Exams are over; hadn't you noticed?"

"I know, but I'm interested. Might even catch up with some sleep too – I've been having these dreams..."

"Wolves," teased Amy. "Yes, we know. You terrified Hannah." She added in a schoolmistressy voice: "The last wolf left this part of Europe over two hundred years ago."

"How do you know?"

"Because I checked," she confessed. "Because the name of the house scared me."

I set myself up on the lawn with some ancient magazines and a couple of kids' storybooks.

Amy gawped. "My God, she's serious!"

Mum squatted beside me with a glass of water and a couple of aspirins. "Sure you'll be all right, love?"

I eyed her sternly. "Don't flap, Mother."

"And eat something, do," called Martine. "There's salami in the fridge. Help yourself."

I gave up on the French and just looked at the pictures. "Bye, Ellie," called Hannah. Then I stretched out on my back in the sunlit grass. I could hear the doors of the Volvo slamming on already remote voices, the horn calling farewell as the car rounded the bend – *toot-toot; toot-toot*... I looked up and the house seemed to open all its eyes and gaze down at me. Mine. It was mine.

I drifted and dozed and woke up with mosquito bites. The shadow of the walls had swallowed up all my sun. I took myself inside. I was suddenly empty, ravenous.

I brought out the salami, but the bread in the basket was dry and brittle. In the high cupboard I found the spaghetti we'd bought – that would do. I half lifted a saucepan, then looked across at the row of ancient pots and pans. The temptation was too great. A hornet's nest? I was prepared to risk it.

The pot was heavy but, struggling, I scrubbed it free of its cobwebs and grime. Filled with water, it seemed to weigh a ton. When the pasta was cooked, I strained it through a colander and slopped it triumphantly on to a plate.

I stirred it up with butter and grated cheese and tucked into it solemnly, messily, elbows on the table. The kitchen was sunless and sombre now, my orange and pink shorts a shock of rude colour. A small lizard went zigzagging up the whitewashed wall and a pale butterfly, drifting in like a lost ballerina, began fluttering dizzily round my head.

I moved away. Nature, I thought. Too many winged things, too many scuttling things. I washed up my plate, left the pot to soak, and went off, exchanging the smell of melted butter and windfall apples for the churchy fragrance of old books, the musty tang of ancient drapes and the warm perfume of flowers drifting in through the windows. I remember wandering in a trance, not knowing whether I was awake or asleep, watching a housefly making a trail across a red and green fleur-de-lis and running my fingers over the blue and gold robes of the statue of Ste Anne.

The rhyme came from nowhere: "Sainte Anne, Sainte Anne, send me a man." I don't need one, I thought; I've got Alain.

And I lingered in front of the big bay windows, making a box with my fingers the way our art teacher had taught us, framing the gold and the black, the shell-pink and the blue; mauve shadows on green.

There were pastels in my room.

But on the way up I began looking for the dolls instead, opening wardrobes and cupboards, even drawers (*Maman* would not have approved of this disorder). And some were still there, with their parted rosy lips, their front teeth like rice grains, their curled cotton wool hair, and those flower-sprigged dresses too precious ever to be played with.

And I went up still further to look in Amy's room, but it wasn't Amy's, it was Suzanne's and what was that housemaid doing with my clothes? I took out my one grand dress – bought when I was just sixteen and they wanted to marry me off – and held it against me. Then I lifted it over my head and let it fall over that silly vest and those cut-price knickers, and felt the silk brushing against the calves of my legs.

Bare legs. . . there should have been silk stockings. I went off to find them, foxtrotting down the corridor and into his room, his shrine. They'd let the candle burn down under his portrait – my only love, I'm here now. I opened the wardrobe. Disorder again. Boxes. Hatboxes. *À la mode des demoiselles Martignon* (those two elderly virgins, what did they ever know?).

I kept my silky stockings in a blue velvet bag.

I tipped out the boxes but they were full of junk – papers, letters, photographs, souvenirs. Souvenirs. *Je souviens. . .* I found a plait of hair, my own long hair before I had it bobbed. Then the lonely wolf cried out to me from beyond the long shadows and I responded, running downstairs and straight into Angus.

He caught me. He held me.

Then he kissed me.

CHAPTER NINE

The others turned up noisily just before seven.

Amy's hair was witch-wild. "It was so windy! Windy and hot. You should have come."

"Look what I bought," squealed Hannah, waving a small floury corn sheaf made out of bread dough.

"You'll never eat that," I said. This was the kid who felt guilty about tucking into a milk chocolate bunny.

Hannah looked offended. "I'm not going to. I'll take it home and put it on the wall of my room."

"Our room," I reminded her.

Martine glanced at me quickly and her face was one big question mark.

"Oh, Angus came back," I said airily. "He's upstairs, sleeping it off."

"The slob," said Martine, but I could see she was relieved.

Mum sat down at the table and lit herself a cigarette. "You feeling better love?"

I reached for the packet. "I'll have one with you," I said, watching her face. I took out a fag. "Give me a light."

Mum sat there with her mouth open. "You're too young," she said weakly.

"Oh, come on!"

"You're a bad example, Chrissie," scolded Martine, who'd given up. "Maybe Ellie's trying to tell you something."

At that point Mum blew her top: "Ellie! Take that thing out of your mouth!" and I did, I did. When Mum was in that mood, you just did what she told you.

She tore a strip off Martine too. "You don't live under my kinds of pressures so don't be so patronizing!"

"Hey you three – stop it!" said Amy, who couldn't stand rows.

I will never know what made me say it: "We can get mad if we want to. We're not all like your lot!" The minute it was out I was horrified.

Amy jerked as if I'd slapped her. Then she ran off upstairs.

"Ellie!" Mum looked really shocked. "That was uncalled for!"

"Think I don't know?" That stupid kiss had unnerved me; Angus had no right to come barging into my fantasy. I must have been dreaming, half asleep, and he'd taken advantage. "That dress," he'd explained lamely. "Thought you were a ghost. Sorry, Ellie – I must still be a bit pissed..." I suppose you'd have to be, I thought furiously, to want to kiss me.

I went up to Amy and found her in tears.

"I'm sorry."

"Get lost," she snuffled.

"I didn't mean it."

"Oh, yes you did!" She mopped her cheeks with the corner of the sheet. "What's wrong with my parents anyway? What's wrong with being just ordinary? Not everyone's dad can get a book published."

She was envious? Of me?

Shaken, I sat down beside her. "And not everyone's dad has a girlfriend not much older than us."

"Oh, Ellie, I know, I know." She put an arm round me. "That must hurt a lot, but you never talk about it."

I clammed up at once. "What's there to talk about? Men are like that."

"Not all men."

Well, not Alain, I thought; he'd have been faithful. But then he came from another age. "It's to do with the pill," I said stupidly.

Amy looked baffled. "What is?"

"I mean, if Penny got pregnant I don't think he'd like her any more. Steve never went much for babies and messes."

Amy sighed.

"I love all the messes in your place, Ellie. All those fabric bits and gold stuff and sequins, and the way your mum makes it all work. She's a great influence on me, your mum – did you know that?" (I couldn't imagine my mum being an influence on anyone.) "She's so tough and so clever." (I was amazed.) "She's partly why I've decided to try for Drama."

"Mum is? You're kidding!"

"No, I'm not."

"She's so untidy. We eat off trays half the time, because the table's always covered with her stuff. Drove my dad crazy."

Amy frowned. "It wasn't just that though, was it? It couldn't have been. I mean, they must have been incompatible. Did they row much?"

I remembered; the memory still hurt. "Yes," I said briefly.

"I'm sorry," said Amy. "That must have been hell." She paused. "But I thought it was only people like accountants and bank managers who wanted things tidy. And housewives. I mean, my mum's always dusting and tidying things away but she doesn't do anything else. Your dad's creative."

"But with a soul like a filing cabinet." I liked the sound of that phrase, but it wasn't quite fair. I quickly changed the subject.

"I'm in love," I blurted.

Amy looked alarmed. "Does he know?"

"Does who know?"

"Angus."

I laughed. I'd already forgotten Angus and his clumsy kiss. "Oh, not him!"

"Then who?"

"I can't tell you." I'd told her far too much already. Enough to push her into nagging at me: "Who, then? Who?"

* * *

Mum did supper that night. "Your turn tomorrow."

"OK," we sighed. "OK."

Angus came down late, pale, blinking, his pink-rimmed eyes carefully avoiding mine.

Martine gave him a sharp look. "The perfume of Chrissie's meatballs revives even the dead, it seems." She opened a bottle of wine.

Angus groaned. "I'll have water."

"A good evening, then, evidently."

After supper, faking fatigue, I ducked out of a fourth round of backgammon. Going up to my room had become like going to a secret lover. Above my bed, Alain looked down at me, unchanging, mysterious, desirable...

In the wardrobe mirror I watched myself undressing, hating the squidgy mound of my stomach, that pink pound of flesh I could squeeze between finger and thumb. Then I lay back against the pillows, trying to ignore the faint whine of a mosquito, the pirouetting of will o' the wisps above the lamp and the fluttering of yet another moth intent on death by burning. In love? I had a crush on a photograph and that was all.

Something shocked me out of a dreamless doze. Someone was calling me. Was it Amy? Was it Hannah? I sat up and listened. The mournful sound seemed to come drifting in through the slots in the shutters. Some farm dog, Mum had said. Maybe Jules?

This time I got out of bed, pushed the shutters open and looked down into the night garden.

Beyond the moon-washed lawn lay the shadowy trees.

Then once again I heard it and it wasn't a dog...

We drove down to St Brévin to please Hannah – she'd asked for a different beach.

Angus came too, chastened, not saying much. I guessed Martine had had a go at him.

We moved along endless, sandy roads. We meandered through streets of small holiday shanties where beach towels hung like flags under a salty sun, and tourists pedalled solemnly alongside us in comic, bicycle-powered buggies.

The souvenir shops in St Brévin were already packing away their postcard stands and their buckets and spades, their fishing nets on long poles, their pink-framed sun-glasses and their necklaces of shells. It was lunchtime.

Martine squeezed the Volvo into the last available space and we wriggled out.

"This is an extravagance," fretted Mum. "We ought to have done a picnic."

"You're on holiday, Chrissie," said Martine. "Remember?"

We began dawdling like everyone else, comparing menus and prices, and when a half a dozen people vacated a table at Le Snack, we grabbed it.

"Can I have some more of that super-duper drink?" demanded Hannah.

"If you ask for it," challenged Martine. "Go on. Dare you." She spelt it out phonetically.

"Gru – na – deen."

Angus winked at her. "Go on, Hannah – you can do it."

One of the buggies we'd seen on the way in sailed ridiculously past, its two drivers pedalling furiously.

"Those things expensive?" said Amy. "I'd love to have a go."

"I'll treat you," said Angus. Then he seemed to remember me, Ellie, sitting like a dead weight over a glass of red wine. "You too, Ellie."

"Two's company," I said coldly and saw him flush. Got you, I thought.

"Me! Me!" Hannah suggested discreetly.

"Oh, Hannah," sighed Mum.

When we got to the ice-cream, Martine said, "Why don't you lot book your ride now? We can wait for you here. More amusing than sitting in the car."

When they'd taken themselves off, Mum said, "You're in an odd mood, Eleanor Portman. Why didn't you go with them?"

"Why should I?" I countered. "I can't always do what you expect."

"Well, neither can I." She took out a cigarette and lit it. "So don't nag me."

Martine called the waitress.

"*Trois cafés, mademoiselle.*"

I considered bringing up the wolf topic again, now that Hannah had left, but suspected I'd get the same reaction. Martine was hiding something, I knew. I'd never heard a dog make a sound like that.

So I tried something else. "Are there any photograph albums in the house?" Alain, I thought. Alain.

"I should think so, yes. The problem would be finding them."

"Could we look? I'd love to see you as a little kid," I lied.

"There won't be many of me," said Martine. "I never went there much as a child. It was just after the war, you see; things were – difficult."

I hadn't thought of anything like that. "Were you in it?" I asked inanely. "The war, I mean."

"I was a kid," said Martine. "But I remember it, just. The Germans dug up the tennis courts."

"Were there tennis courts?" asked Mum.

"There used to be, back in the Thirties. Where Monsieur Auguste has his vegetable garden."

Amy and Angus returned with Hannah skipping between them.

"That was wowee!" chirped Hannah. "I mean that was superfrabdigious."

Martine frowned. "That's a word I don't know," she said. "And after all these years."

Mum giggled. "Neither does anyone else. Hannah made it up."

"Oh, you are clever," said Martine, and Hannah looked smug.

We drove down to the long strip of a beach, parking under the inadequate shade of a gangly pine. I took off my shorts and boldly rolled down the top of my swimsuit. If Angus wanted an eyeful, I thought, turning on to my stomach, it was all there.

Hannah trotted off for a swim with Mum and Martine. I shimmied out a soft hollow under the beach towel and lay inside it, the sun roasting my back. My head turned to one side, I regarded Amy's profile – the dark bushy eyebrows she was always plucking, the brown mole on her cheek, the large nose that she hated and the full, sensuous mouth.

"I can see billions of atoms," she was saying. I could see her lashes fluttering. "All vibrating, spinning. . ."

"You can't see an atom," said Angus, "with the naked eye."

"Well some of us can." She rolled over to face me, turning her back on him. "Your mum's going to visit the old lady tomorrow," she said. "They're both going."

"What old lady? You mean Martine's aunt?'

"Great aunt," Amy corrected.

I considered it lazily. "Do we all go?"

"Well, I should, I suppose," said Angus. "I usually do."

"Where does she live?"

"St Nazaire," he said. "*Une maison de retraite.*"

Amy sat up. "Stop showing off! We all know you're bilingual. If you mean an old people's home, why don't you say so?"

I thought – why did she always pick on him?

Martine splashed out of the sea and came trotting up the beach with Hannah and Mum. "It's going to rain," she announced happily as she stretched out beside me like a fat, wet seal.

I blinked up at my own dancing motes,

speckling the blue. "Out of that sky?"

"You haven't seen the haze. No horizon – look."

Hannah squatted, spreading a wet bruise over the sand.

I wrapped my arms round my knees and gazed down at the sea, at the white curls of foam and the restless green-grey contours slip-slopping into nothingness.

"There used to be a town out there, so they say," said Martine dreamily. "Montoise. Then the sea rose up and swallowed it."

"And if you come down here at the right time," said Angus, "you can hear the church bells ringing under the water."

"When is the right time?" asked Hannah eagerly.

"Some time when the two worlds come close enough to mesh."

"Oh, Angus, you're such a romantic," said Martine fondly.

"You believe that stuff?" I asked him. "Different worlds?"

"Or alternative versions of this one."

"That might explain ghosts," I said sharply, and he had the decency to blush.

CHAPTER
TEN

I made a deal with Martine. She'd hunt out photographs and I'd cook supper. ("That's no deal,"
Mum narked. "It was your turn anyway.")

Amy went with me as galley slave. "I'm hopeless
at cooking," she said, watching me making a stock
for the risotto. "My mother never lets any of us
near the stove – says it's quicker and less mess
to do it herself."

"Well, I never had much choice," I said, running
water over the rice. "I mean, Hannah was too
little, and with Mum always working it wouldn't
have been fair."

Outside, as Martine had predicted, the sky
had thickened to an ochreous grey. It was as
if someone had switched off all the lights.
We had to switch ours on – two brown-
spotted bulbs inside a halo of mites.

"Why are you so keen on seeing those old
photos?"

I side-stepped. "Well aren't you?" Inside

Martine's big plastic apron I could feel myself sweating. "I mean, we've seen so much of their family's stuff – wouldn't it be nice to look at some of the people?"

Amy rinsed the chopping board. "You looked fabulous in that dress."

"Thank you."

"Like someone else."

"Thanks a million."

"My pleasure." She grinned. "Heard any more wolves?" Outside, the telephone rang a few times, then stopped. "One of the girlfriends, bet you."

"Can't think why they bother."

"I don't know. He's quite sexy, don't you think?"

"Not my type."

"So who is?" taunted Amy. "Why don't you tell me? I'd tell you."

I swooshed the rice into the hot oil.

"OK, OK," she joked. "If that's how you feel about it."

After supper we followed Martine into the Sainte Anne room. Over the thin sage rug she'd spread two or three sombre-looking albums with squiggly gold lettering.

"This was all I could find," she said, arranging herself squarely on the floor. "Hope it will do. Ellie, that risotto was..." and she brought the tip of her finger to meet her thumb in a big O, "*parfait!*" She picked up one of the books and started turning the pages. "This is me, look, that little girl with her *papa*."

Hannah dug her chin into Martine's shoulder.

"Where was your mum?"

"Oh, she didn't often come to Chanteloup. They didn't really approve of her."

"Why not?" Hannah asked.

Martine shrugged. "She was half Arab and proud. They used to label her "native" and she didn't like it."

"I should think not," said Mum.

"Bunch of bloody racists, Mum's lot," teased Angus.

"You can't say that," Martine argued. "Times were different. Conventions were different. Anyway, old Henriette used to stick up for her."

"Alain wouldn't have said anything like that . . ." The words were out before I could stop them.

"Oh, I'm not so sure. Anyway, he wasn't around by then. Died back in the Thirties." She gave me a hard look. "Alain's really got to you, hasn't he?"

The rose-coloured lampshade neutralized my pink cheeks. "I *am* sleeping in his room."

Martine fanned back some pages. "Well, here is your Alain." She pointed out a formal family group – unsmiling mum and dad lording it over their offspring.

"They all look like girls," said Hannah.

"Well, little kids did then," said Mum. "You should see some of our old snaps."

I concentrated on the face Martine had picked out for me, the solemn child in a sailor suit and dark beret, his arm protectively round a toddler in white.

Martine smiled. "That baby's my great-aunt."

"Henriette?"

"That's right." She turned a page. "Here she is again, a bit older."

The girl in the photograph could have been eleven or twelve, and her face, above a long white dress with elaborately puffed sleeves, was set into one of Hannah's knowing half smiles. Her hair was long and dark and parted in the middle, but under soft, barely-marked brows, her eyes seemed to burn.

Amy sighed enviously. "She looks like an angel."

"Oh, she was no angel," said Martine. "I can tell you that."

I wondered if I'd recognize her. She'd be... "How old is she now?"

"*Tatie* Henriette? Pushing ninety – must be." Then Martine was off. "And here's my grandmother..." I began to lose track of those almost identical charcoal-grey snapshots. "And here's Alain in uniform..." I leaned forward. "They sent the two boys off to some priests' academy. Didn't bother about the girls, of course." She turned another page. "Oh, look. Alain and Henriette. She must be about fifteen in this one." My eyes slipped past the girl in a tennis dress to absorb every smudged detail of that tall young man posing self-consciously with his younger sister.

"Twenties style still," pronounced Mum expertly. "Cut off all that pretty hair – wanted to look like a boy. And is she underdeveloped or did she tie up her boobs in a binder?"

"In a what?"

"They had to be flat, you see. The erogenous zone was the pudenda."

"She means the fanny," I explained to Amy, "but she's too polite to say so."

I nurtured my freshly-planted memories, and by the time I went up to bed the portrait already seemed to have grown new depths. I was beginning to feel as if I'd known him all my life. Yet I knew almost nothing.

So before going to sleep I amused myself by making things up, inventing a romantic past for him. He'd wanted to be a painter; those were Alain's pastels in the alcove, untouched, and why? They wouldn't let him. They'd sent him off to that priests' school. Bunch of racists, I thought. So no imagination. They wouldn't have wanted an artist in the family. They'd have wanted him to be – what? A lawyer? A doctor? Maybe a priest. Of course the guy'd rebelled.

And then he'd fallen in love with the wrong girl. Maybe with a servant. They would have sent her packing – the old class thing again. Or maybe with one of Henriette's friends, haughty, dismissive. Females can be bitches.

Against the slant of the shutters, rain began falling in a quickening patter, like waves pummelling a rock. And the drowning, I thought. Perhaps it hadn't been an accident. All or nothing, that was my Alain.

I threw myself with him over the cliff, looked up and saw that fontanelle of water closing over my eyes, felt my own mouth filling with salt and heard through my blocked ears the muffled wail of a distant foghorn . . . if you dream you're dead you'll never wake up . . .

I struggled to the surface. I was hot, I was sweating, but the room was all round me, solid, real, the feather mattress in damp, billowing mounds, the rough wool of the blanket scratching me through a hole in the sheet that shouldn't have been there.

And from somewhere outside the wolf was calling.

There *is* a wolf, I thought crossly. I can prove it.

Still stupid with sleep, I got out of bed and tiptoed down to Amy's room, switching on the light over the engraving of the bloke who got blown up with his ship. "Amy," I whispered, but she moaned and blotted out the glare with a sheet. I considered shaking her awake, then thought better of it. I pushed back the switch and stood in the dark, listening.

Silence. Nothing. The wretched beast would have let me down anyway.

Frustrated, I went back to my own room and pushed open the shutters. "*Owoooo!*" I called flippantly.

"*Owooo,*" I heard, faintly, like an echo. "*Owooo . . .*"

I banged the shutters closed and groped back into bed, my heart beating overtime. I lay there, blinking into the blinding dark. It couldn't fly, could it? It couldn't get at me?

Better a wolf outside, I joked feebly, than a moth inside. . .

"Angus and I must go to visit Henriette," Martine announced next morning. "Chrissie's coming too. You lot can stay here if you like; there's plenty to do and lots of good walks if you don't mind the rain. But you might enjoy the ride. I can't promise you any sparkling conversation – Henriette's lost most of her teeth and can't be bothered with dentures. But there's always the town; we could have tea afterwards."

"I'm staying," said Hannah firmly. "I want to go on Margot again."

"I'll come," I said quickly. (Henriette had known him, touched him.)

"I'm easy," said Amy.

"Not too easy, I hope."

"Oh, Mum," I said, seeing Amy go pink. "What a thing to say!" Mum can be so embarrassing sometimes.

Angus picked out a carrot from the vegetable box. "Take Margot this," he said, offering it to Hannah. "She likes carrots. But then you come with us. You can't stay here by yourself."

"But Monsieur Auguste will be around," argued Hannah cleverly.

"Monsieur Auguste," said Martine, "will be busy." She turned to Angus. "By the way, have you done something about Saturday night?"

"I think so – yes." He turned to us awkwardly. "They've been asked out," he said. "The two mothers."

"Those two?" joked Amy. "Now who'd do a thing like that?"

But I'd already guessed.

"Guy's taking them to a restaurant in Nantes."

"Great," I said coldly. I turned to Mum like a stern governess. "So what about Hannah?"

"What about Hannah?" asked Hannah.

Angus cleared his throat nervously.

"I thought – if you'd like it – that we'd go out with Edouard in the jeep."

"Yes, please," said Hannah.

"Gilles is doing a small gig at the Café Robert over in St Michel."

Martine frowned. "That wierdo..."

"And he'd like a bit of support."

"Just try to stop us," said Amy.

"Won't it be late?" I said cautiously. "For Hannah, I mean?"

"I don't mind," said Hannah. "I can stay up until morning."

"Is that OK, Ellie?" I saw the pleading in Mum's eyes and I nodded dumbly. So you are zee dress designer... She'd soon get fed up with that sort of crap.

"Your mum needs a little outing now and again," observed Martine.

I bristled. "Well, we don't stop her."

Outside it was lowering and humid, much hotter than it had been in the house. I placed myself next to Amy in the back of the Volvo. The sun was an orange haze in a fork of sullen cloud.

Martine began carolling something from one of those operas. Irritated, I began needling her.

"Do you do that when you're drilling teeth?"

She stopped singing. "All the time," she said cheerfully.

"Isn't that a bit sadistic?"

"But dentists are sadists, Ellie. Didn't you know that?" and she began warbling: "*Behold the Lord High Executioner...*"

Oh, she's so superficial, I thought.

The first raindrops hit the windscreen and the wipers began scraping across the glass with the faint whine of a high-speed drill.

I continued with my attack.

"How did Alain drown?" I asked, expecting one of her vague, evasive replies.

"By tying a weight to his body, I presume."

"Oh, Ellie," wailed Mum.

I was shocked too, but I couldn't stop. "So he killed himself?"

"That's right."

"Why?"

Mum said, "Ellie, that's enough. It's none of your business."

"Would you like to change your room?" asked Martine.

"Not particularly. Why?"

She hesitated. "Because sometimes Alain has this effect on people," she said at last. "And it's not healthy. I'm worried about you."

"Well don't be." My face felt hot. "I'm just curious that's all. His photograph *is* over my bed." I suddenly realized how appalling I'd just been. "I'm sorry," I said. "I shouldn't have gone on like that."

"I should think not," said Mum.

"I'm not curious about that guy who blew himself up," said Amy. "And he's over *my* bed."

"Well, he's not sexy," I said, struggling to reduce the conversation to a trivial level.

"True, true."

"I'd be curious about *him*, too," I lied, "if I had him. You know me."

"Yes, I do." Amy laughed. "If you can't dig out a good story about someone, you make one up. You'll end up as a reporter for the *News of the World*."

"*The Sun*," I joked. "*If* you please!"

"I'm going to be a Page Three girl," said Hannah.

"Not if I've got anything to do with it," said Mum.

"What would you really like to do?" asked Angus.

"Me?" I said. "Dunno. Write, possibly. Seems to run in the family."

"I'm going to act," declared Amy.

"That's a tough job," said Angus. "Even when you've got talent."

Amy stiffened. "Are you suggesting I haven't?"

Rain dribbled from the green-grey curves of the iron railings and flattened the Smartie-coloured petals of busy Lizzies and geraniums.

The matron of the old people's home was youngish and brisk and we dutifully shook hands with her.

"*Bonjour*," said Hannah, showing off her French.

The old lady was sitting in a wheelchair, a pink baby blanket tucked round her shoulders.

"*Tatie Henriette!*" Martine kissed her on both cheeks. "*Mes amis anglais.*"

I looked for the burning eyes, but they were distorted by spectacles. Her eyebrows, still sparse, were now white, and the thin layer of scraped-back hair revealed the tender shell of her scalp. Her skin was so textured with lines it looked as if it had always been that way. She was the oldest person I'd ever seen and she was like a different species. A turtle. A lizard.

She regarded us blankly. Then her gaze fixed on Angus. Suddenly her fingers stopped plucking at the fluff on her skirt and she grabbed at his wrist, jerked back her frail head, parted her pink gums and howled like a wolf.

I stepped back, horrified.

A nurse hurried over and began stroking her head. "*Oh, comme vous êtes méchante devant votre si gentille famille...*" The howl subsided into a hum and then into a mutter as the old lady relaxed her grip. Martine bent close to listen. "*Pas Alain, ma tante,*" she whispered. "Angus!" She pronounced it *On goose.* "*Mon fils.*"

I felt shocked. Angus? Like Alain? I thought about it. They shared the same roots... I looked at him afresh, but could find no similarity. He was too young and his hair was the wrong colour.

I turned back to the old lady. Alain's sister. She had known him, touched him; she could have told me so much if she hadn't been potty. I struggled with my French, but the words in my head refused to be herded into a meaningful sentence and I could only smile at her dumbly.

Did she hear wolves too?

Did Martine? Did Angus? Was it catching?

Martine made her offerings – a tin of Sainsbury's shortbread and a small book wrapped loosely in blue tissue paper. Something religious, I assumed, or sentimental. Maybe photos – the sort of things my own gran would like.

The book tumbled out into Henriette's lap and Martine turned the pages for her to see.

I peeped and caught a glimpse of whirling colours, tortured landscapes. "Van Gogh," I said, surprised.

Martine smiled and nodded. "She was keen on art."

I looked at Henriette guiltily. Just then I'd been making assumptions, labelling her "Old Lady" when she was a real person. Suddenly the white hair and wrinkles became irrelevant: she was Alain's sister again and I wanted to hug her.

It went on raining all evening.

"I'm bored," complained Hannah after Amy'd beaten her at draughts for the third time. "Wish there was a telly."

"If there was, you wouldn't understand it."

"Yes, I would," said Hannah stubbornly.

"There's a game we play here sometimes," said Martine, "but it needs props. Give me a hand, Chrissie?"

"What game?" I asked Angus.

"Wait and see."

They came back with armfuls of clothes, hats, scarves, even shoes. They must have ransacked the place. Mum sparkled like a kid. She loved dressing up.

"Charades," she announced.

"Wow," said Amy, running her fingers over a velveteen gipsy dress with half a dozen petticoats. "This is the real stuff."

"Depends what you mean by that," said Martine. "Some of it has always been dress-up. Like that one."

We split into two teams. I felt about five, but secretly I was enjoying it.

"English or French?" said Angus and Amy hit him with a straw hat.

Mum and Martine came on as awful school kids, with Hannah as the teacher. Then Martine did a wicked stepmother with Hannah as the child and Mum as the good fairy. Our lot did a heart-rending version of Marie Antoinette having her head chopped off, followed by a sketch of a long-suffering bloke going shopping with two extravagant daughters.

"You *have* got talent," said Angus.

"I know," purred Amy.

We dug out a couple of Twenties dresses. Amy's wouldn't hook up at the back.

Angus went on in shorts. "Who's for tennis?" he asked, waving a ping-pong bat.

"*Moi*," declared Amy, slapping him with a feather boa.

"*Et moi*," I said, swinging a beaded evening bag.

Then Angus clapped his hand over his heart.
"*Mon amour*," he said, turning to Amy.
"*Je t'aime*," hammed Amy. She glanced sideways
at me. "*Alain*," she added wickedly, giving Angus
a long, lingering kiss.

CHAPTER
ELEVEN

"Kiss, kiss," smirked Hannah.

"Oh, Hannah," wailed Mum.

"Can't think what made me do that," Amy said lightly, her eyes still fixed on Angus's face.

"All part of the charade," said Martine, looking worldly-wise.

"We give up," said Mum. "Tell us the word."

"Oooh!" Amy faked shock. "We forgot to say it!"

"We won, we won," crowed Hannah. "Knew we would." She pointed at us. "They're hopeless."

The game disintegrated and Amy wandered off. After a while I went upstairs and found her sitting on her bed, weaving strands of her hair into little plaits.

"What made you do that?"

She frowned. "I was trying to get it to go into waves..."

"I don't mean your hair."

"Oh, him?" Pulling a thin braid across her face, she squinted past it. "I don't know. Does it matter?"

"Not really."

"Something got into me. Role playing, I suppose." Amy was into psychology. "We've talked about this before. You should try it; it's fun." She sighed. "I felt like a Thirties vamp, out of one of those old movies."

"Oh, come off it, Amy. You really embarrassed him."

"Did I?" She licked the end of the braid and fastened it off with a rubber band.

I fell apart. "For God's sake, Amy. There are other things in life besides sex."

"Are there?" She looked up at me, huge-eyed and innocent. "Like what?"

I wanted to scream. Why did she have to act like that? I turned away. "See you tomorrow." She was laughing at me, I knew. "Too much sex rots your mind," I said virtuously.

In my own room I propped open the shutters and sat listening to the warm rain bouncing off the Virginia creeper. I thought about Amy; I thought about Steve. Love didn't last; neither did friendship. Then I gazed over at Alain, unchanged since the Thirties; I could come back in ten years and he'd still look at me like that.

Inside the crimson glass pot I found the stub of a night-light and a couple of dead flies; what a mess, I thought as I tipped them out. I took a new night-light from the half-used packet in the alcove. The wick caught at the third try. I grinned. Watch it, Alain, I thought: you're really a saint now.

Oddly comforted by that little red glow, I

undressed and got into bed. For a while I read by lamplight, trying to ignore the thin whine of a mosquito somewhere in the room. I switched off the lamp, but over my head the warm flame flickered. It made me feel safe. It made me feel bold. Now's your chance, Mr Wolf, I joked. Come and get me...

Instantly a cry shattered the silence of the night, plaintive, hypnotic. "*Oowooo...*"

"*Ooowoo!*" I repeated cynically.

"*Oowoo,*" it howled.

I got out of bed and latched the shutters tight. I had started to shiver.

My door creaked open. "Ellie? You all right?" Someone switched on the light.

I blinked. "No, I'm not. There's a wolf out there."

Angus grinned.

"You mean, there's a wolf in here."

I suddenly felt like a fool.

"I was dreaming," I said crossly. "That's all."

I heard it last night," announced Amy next morning. "Your wolf."

Hannah's eyes widened.

"Not a real wolf?"

Mum frowned at Amy. "There aren't any wolves," she said. "Amy's just having you on."

"Who's afraid," chortled Martine, "of the big bad wolf?" but her eyes regarded me questioningly. Martine knew something, but she wasn't telling.

I jabbed a vague question into that bosomy façade. "How come your aunty likes Van Gogh?"

107

Martine looked puzzled. "Why shouldn't she? Lots of people do."

But I needed to give more depth to my fantasy.

"Did Alain paint?"

Martine smiled. "No, but Henriette did. Those two landscapes in the dining room are hers and there are sketchbooks somewhere too. I must find them and show you." She gave me an odd look. "It was probably Henriette who took the photograph in your room. She was interested in photography. There was a much older brother who was a professional, kept a darkroom, and she used to borrow some of his equipment."

But I didn't want to hear about a much older brother. "So what did Alain do?" If I had to re-invent his past, I needed some input.

"Aren't you nosy?" said Hannah.

Angus came in, bleary-eyed, half-asleep. I prayed he'd say nothing and he didn't. Martine poured him a bowl of coffee. "Good afternoon," she teased. Then she turned to the rest of us. "We ought to go out for some bread or there won't be any."

We drove down to St Père and bought baguettes, stacking them on the back seat between Amy and me. Hannah reached over and broke off a crust. "Mmm," she said. "Still warm."

"Why don't we swim?" said Amy when we got back.

I looked at the grey sky. "In this weather?"

"If you're wet already it doesn't make any difference."

"So what about drying?"

"Plenty of big towels," said Martine. "And a warm car. I'll take us all over to St Michel."

"I'm not coming," said Hannah. "I want to ride."

"Well, Angus will be around and Marie-Luce is coming over with Cathérine," said Martine. "So I suppose you could this time."

"Poor Margot," sighed Mum.

Towards evening a glimmer of gold marked the edge of the weather. We watched it spreading, shredding the clouds and drowning the sky in a sunset lake.

"Fine day tomorrow," Martine remarked.

We spent part of that evening with the Augustes and Marie-Luce, drinking Crème de Cassis out of thimble-sized glasses. M. Auguste beamed up at the clear sky.

"Jollee nice," he observed wisely.

Marie-Luce was chatting to Martine.

"Marie-Luce says there's a steam fair," translated Martine. "Tomorrow. Over at St Père. We'll go, shall we? Ought to be fun."

We trailed back to the house in a small procession.

Martine nudged Angus. "Your turn to cook tonight, *mon fils*. Unless you've got other plans."

"I feel tiddly," declared Amy.

Angus chuckled. "That's Mme Auguste's Crème de Cassis. Says it's medicinal. For her chest. Swears she'd never touch a drop of spirits."

We crowded into the kitchen.

"Want some help?" offered Amy. "I'm a good galley slave. Ask Ellie."

"I can manage," said Angus stiffly.

"I'm a super chopper," said Hannah.

"OK," said Angus with resignation. "Stick around."

"We know when we're not wanted," said Amy. She turned to me. "Come on, Ellie."

"Where?"

"Surprise."

I followed her reluctantly between the ridges of vegetables. Rain still beaded the crinkly lettuce leaves and damp earth wormed into our plastic jelly-shoes.

The tied twigs dripped water on to our backs as we entered the bush house. The wet leaves smelt astringent, metallic. Amy squeezed herself into one of the kindergarten chairs. "Good, isn't it?" She looked so funny down there, like an overblown gnome, that I started a giggle. Amy caught it and for a few moments we were helpless. I hadn't laughed like that for ages and the taste of it was like honey.

"I did hear your wolf last night," she spluttered, and that set me off again.

"What's so funny?" she gasped.

"Nothing," I said, catching her eye to keep the giggle going for a little bit longer. It was just like old times. I said suddenly, "I don't want to grow up."

"Oh, I do," said Amy, offering me some of her chocolate. "Anyway, you've got no choice."

"I know," I said dismally.

"I want freedom," said Amy. "Don't you? And my own place, even if it's a dump. And I want to try out different ways of being. I mean, I love my family, but I don't want to be like them."

"I don't want to be much like Mum," I confided. "I mean, she never grew up." I suddenly realized what I'd said, but Amy hadn't noticed. "And she still hankers after Steve." I hoped that wasn't true, but it sounded respectable.

"Let's take the boat out," said Amy. "Tonight."

"We ought to ask," I said nervously.

"We will, fusspot." Amy sighed. "What's the matter with you, Ellie? You're such a wimp these days. You used to be much more fun."

"So did you," I said, "before you turned into a vamp."

We laid the table in the dining-room.

Angus brought in the artichokes, serving them up on a pewter fish plate.

"Even *he* can cook," groaned Amy. "Now I'll have to learn."

We dipped the stems into lemon-flavoured mayonnaise.

"Delicious," said Mum. "You should open a restaurant."

I began studying the two pictures on the opposite wall, a meadow with poppies, and a wild seascape. I hadn't really noticed them before.

Amy said, "That boat. The one that's tied to a willow. Can we take it out some time?"

Martine shrugged. "If you want to. It should be OK, but you need to check. And do be careful – that lake is deep. One of my cousins drowned in it."

111

Amy took a second helping of lamb chops with rosemary. "We can swim."

"Not Hannah," said Mum quickly.

"Yes, I can," said Hannah. "I got my green badge."

Amy's eyes met mine. Let's do it, they said. "When they're all asleep," she whispered as we went upstairs. "Imagine being out on that lake in moonlight..."

"What about the wolf?"

"There isn't any wolf."

"But you said you heard it!" I felt betrayed.

"You knew that was a joke. You laughed, didn't you?"

Yes, I had.

Perhaps I was becoming neurotic, I thought. Too much swotting, too much trying. Amy never seemed to have that problem. "OK," I said reluctantly, still anxious to keep up with her.

"Great. I'll be down to your room in a couple of hours. Don't pass out."

I kicked off my jelly shoes and curled up on my bed. I tried to read, but the words stayed just words. From his pale oval Alain gazed down at me. Approvingly, I told myself: it was just the kind of silly, romantic thing he might have done. I reached up and relit the candle. Then I put out the light and opened the shutters. The night air was warm and scented with grass. I looked out at the dark fringe of trees beyond the moon-powdered lawn. Of course there weren't any wolves. Just farm dogs...

I drew back the shutters, switched on the lamp,

put out a jumper and rolled my swimsuit up in a bath towel. Restless, I pushed open the door and looked along the corridor at the thin line of light that marked Angus's room. We could have invited him too, but it might have been difficult – right now, Amy was so unpredictable. I stretched out on the bed. I yawned. The house creaked and settled. Angus put on some classical tape, piano music, dreamy stuff. Amy'd come soon...

I opened my eyes on a lit room. I'd forgotten to put out the lamp, I thought. Then I remembered. Above my head the candle stub had long since petered out. So where was Amy? I scratched my leg furiously; some insect had bitten me while I'd been sleeping. Smugly I smoothed out my crumpled skirt. So much for Amy. She'd overslept.

I was considering whether I ought to go down to her room when I heard her calling from somewhere outside.

"Ell – eee." Her voice was drifting. "Ell – eee . . . "

What an idiot, I thought. She'll wake everyone up.

I opened the shutters. The lawn was empty.

"Coming," I croaked, committing myself.

Barefoot, I tiptoed down two flights of stairs and across the hall, my fingers brushing the pistachio-coloured surface of the ping-pong table. Then I reached for the door and jiggled back the bolt.

Outside it was warm. I slipped on my shoes and stood, waiting for my eyes to adapt to the dark. Soon I could make out the low stone wall supporting the terrace, then, gradually, the mounded hydrangeas, the chairs and the bone-white table, even the bent straw in Hannah's empty bottle.

I walked down and stood in the damp grass, listening.

"Amy," I whispered loudly. Where was she?

"Ell – ee..."

The voice came from somewhere beyond the meadow.

I gritted my teeth. So she thought I'd chicken out? I'd show her.

I crossed the lawn, stepping boldly in and out of the spread shadows of the chestnut trees. I skirted the pond and opened the gate to the meadow. I could see clearly now. It was like watching one of those black and white films – after a while you forget about colour.

Something heavy and dark blundered out of the gloom of the high hedge. I leapt back and screamed. Margot turned and eyed me mildly, her pupils pinpointed by moonlight. "Oh, Margot," I whimpered, stroking her funny rough coat.

Then: "Amy!" I called, in a hoarse, angry whisper.

"Ell – ee..."

I gazed fearfully across at the black thicket, at the heavy leaves moving against an ashen sky. She was in there somewhere. What the hell was she playing at?

Furious, I strode to the far end of the meadow and plunged into the wood, twigs snapping against my arms and face. Something scampered and fled. Something fluttered against my hair. Damn Amy, I thought; this is not funny.

I reached the edge of the lake with its tiny black island.

"Ell – ee..." I could hear her, but her voice was faint. Had she already taken the boat?

The water was tipped with moonlight.

Suddenly I relaxed. Amy was right. It was magical.

I unrolled my swimsuit from its towelling wrap, but it didn't seem necessary. I took off my clothes and slipped in naked. The water was like silk, like that silk dress I'd felt so good in...

I flailed about for a bit, judging the depth. Then I turned and floated, offering my body to the leaf-dappled moon.

"Ell – ee..."

It didn't matter that she'd got there first. "Coming," I called.

I rolled over and started to swim to the island, slowly, languidly, the spray from my fingers drawing a silver veil over and over my hair. "*Je viens mon amour...*" I felt limp, sexy. The water held me, caressed me. Intimately. "*Je viens; je viens...*"

"Ellie!" The voice came from the shore. "What the hell d'you think you're doing?"

I ignored the girl. She was trivial. She was silly.

"Rat!" shouted Amy. "Why didn't you wait?"

The shadow of the island moved like an arm over my head, drawing me in. I was suddenly frightened. No, I said. No.

I tried to turn round but my arms were too heavy. If I moved forward the swimming was easy, but if I tried to move back I was pushing against a tide. But there wasn't any tide. There couldn't have been.

I heard the creaking of oars.

"Amy!" I called and saw the dark prow of the small boat and the backward trail of foam.

I trod water frantically.

"Hi," she said. "Out for a swim?"

My fingers clung to the rough wood, but I could still feel the water sucking me back. Then her hand was under my elbow, pulling me in.

"You cow," she said admiringly. "Don't drip all over me!"

CHAPTER
TWELVE

I woke up late from a troubled sleep, still trying to work things out. The night's events seemed like a dream – being called by Amy and yet not Amy, feeling the pull of that island and yet being too scared to go ashore.

"What's the point of swimming out to it if you're not going to land?" Amy'd grumbled.

"I don't know." I didn't and it worried me.

"You all right, Ellie? I'm beginning to wonder."

Well, frankly, so was I.

Pushing these conflicts firmly to one side, I got up, reconstructed myself and went downstairs. Amy was sitting alone in the kitchen staring glumly at a copy of *ELLE*. "Make the most of the quiet," she said. "They'll be back soon."

I poured out some coffee and cut a round of baguette. "So where've they all gone?"

"Well, Hannah's out playing with that dog, and Martine and your ma have gone shopping with Angus."

"Do they know about last night?" I asked nervously.

"What's there to tell?" She went back to her magazine.

I took my breakfast out to the lawn and sat gazing across the gold-drenched grass with its sharp-edged shadows to the meadow half circled by woods. A faint odour of decay rose from the pond, souring the sweet scent of flowers, and I remembered that island and shivered.

The Volvo rounded the corner and scraped against gravel. I could hear Martine yelling, "Angus! Get moving!"

Mum came through to the terrace. "Ellie!" she called. "You've got up at last." She came down the steps and squatted beside me. "You and Amy both. What were you up to last night?"

"Nothing much."

She lit a cigarette. She was settling down for a Woman to Woman; I knew all the signs. "What's bugging you about tonight?"

"Tonight?" She'd got me there.

"We're going out with Guy, remember?"

I'd actually forgotten. "Oh, him."

"You don't like him, do you?"

"I don't know him, do I? He's all right, I suppose. Do you fancy him?" If she could ask leading questions, then so could I.

"Oh, Ellie, what nonsense. He's an old friend of Martine's."

"Well, he fancies you."

"That's your over-active imagination again, my girl." But for an instant she looked all silly and shy, like a twelve-year-old who's just been told she's sexy.

"Why wouldn't he fancy you?" I persisted. "Just because Dad's got no taste."

"Oh, Ellie, it isn't that simple. It never was." She sighed. "Are you still feeling abandoned?"

"By Steve? I get to see him, don't I?" I fiddled with my coffee spoon. "It happens to lots of people. We don't have nuclear families any more."

Mum looked at me hard. "Some people do. Like Amy."

"So what?" It didn't affect me.

Mum slid out another cigarette. "Martine's concerned about you," she said, changing tack in midstream. "And I'm a bit worried about Martine."

"Martine?" I was baffled.

"You keep on hassling her. She's convinced you don't like her."

"Oh, that's silly."

"And you keep asking about this guy Alain," she went on. "He died fifty years ago."

"Well, I'm curious."

"Ellie, it isn't personal. I mean, Martine never even knew him. But there are some things people mightn't want to talk about."

"Like suicide?" I challenged. "Listen, that's nothing to be ashamed of. If he'd been around today, someone might have helped him. The Samaritans..."

"That's not the point. Other people's family business is private – unless they choose to share it. You must be old enough to see that."

I plucked out a few blades of grass. "Point taken."

"So keep off the subject." She lit the cigarette she'd been waving about. "It's not healthy."

"Neither," I said, coughing dramatically, "is that."

After lunch we drove over to St Père with the windows open and the sun blinds down. We stepped out on to grass that had been trampled white. Sweat ran down my midriff and soaked into the waistband of my shorts.

Martine bought us raffle tickets.

"What do we get if we win first prize?" asked Hannah.

"An ox."

"Oh, great," said Amy. "Just what I've always wanted. Do you think they'll let us keep it in Laurel Grove Park?"

"We'd have to slaughter it," said Martine. "And roast it over a fire."

"I wouldn't let you," said Hannah, shocked.

"Roast ox," teased Martine. "*Fantastique!*"

"It's a bit academic, isn't it?" said Angus, the realist. "We'd never get it through Customs."

"Then we'd have to eat it here," said Mum. "Anyone for barbecued ox?"

"I'd chat up some lorry driver," said Amy. "I'd get it through." She nudged Angus. "You're a defeatist. Think sideways."

"Seems you do already," said Mum drily.

Martine clapped her hands. "Why do we have to get so serious? I don't know what's happening to us. Must be the weather."

We dawdled, we gaped, stopping to admire the mounds of little biscuits and sweets, the wine, the olives, the pots of honey and the ribboned braids of corn that hung from every stall. Drifts of savoury smoke rose between the oiled and polished mechanical monsters, making my mouth water.

We tucked messily into spare ribs and sweet corn. Then we drifted apart. Angus wandered off and Amy followed him. Then Hannah said, "Ooh look," and she ran over to join the crowd around the steam-powered organ.

Mum nudged me. "Go with her. You don't know who's in that lot."

"Oh, Mum you're so paranoid."

I found Hannah on tiptoe, struggling for a view of the gilded figures, so I let her ride piggy-back on my shoulders. "You weigh a ton," I grumbled. Out of the corner of my eye I could see Amy and Angus visibly quarrelling.

People pressed in on us, scented, sweaty, sticky, smelling of tobacco and barbecue. The sound of their voices, the baying of animals, the rhythmic clanking of the threshing machines and that endless plinky-plonk music must have sent me into some kind of a trance. Two worlds meshing, I thought, and my shoulders ached with the weight of my sister. Then (did I dream it?) we were somewhere else, the big machines rattling past us, puffing steam; heavy horses hauling hay carts; a white cloth spread over trestle tables; harvest — the last sheaf tied with poppies and ribbons, the old songs being sung, the new wine still fermenting on my tongue and his hand in the crowd, reaching secretly for mine – Ellie, Ellie...

"Ellie," called Mum, and I jumped, letting Hannah drop. "Come on! They're announcing the winners."

I blinked. "We won't win," I said. "We never do."

"Well, we might," said Hannah. "Anyway, I want that ox."

"Hannah, have you seen an ox?" Martine pointed out a heavy, wide-horned beast tethered in a pen.

Hannah looked impressed. "I still want one."

"There are other prizes," said Mum, but we left early without any.

"That lot will clog up the roads for hours," said Martine. "And Chrissie and I have a date!"

He called for them on the stroke of seven, punctual, suave and just as creepy.

"Hello, Hannah, Ellie." We shook hands solemnly.

"Saloo, Gee," said Hannah, and Mum looked pleased. She was wearing splashy-print culottes she'd found in Oxfam, with a plain black top and the green stone earrings Dad had once bought her. I gave her a hug to show family solidarity. "You look great," I whispered.

Edouard and Michel turned up quite soon after they'd left. Michel was a vague-looking guy with curly brown hair and spectacles, not Amy's type.

"Where's Gilles?" she asked.

"Oh, he's gone ahead," said Angus, "to set up the sound system."

I played with the idea of opting out again and having that whole scary, magical place to myself, but there was my kid sister and I was supposed to be responsible.

We left at around eight, arranging ourselves on the back seat of the jeep. Familiar with every twist of the road, Edouard drove fast and competently, clipping the hedgerows at each corner.

Hannah was ecstatic. "Faster!" she urged.

Edouard grinned. "*Tu es folle.* We kill ourselves. You too!"

In the Café Robert we sat around green and black rattan tables. Edouard checked on the turnout. "*Pas mal*," he mused. "People here begin to like his music."

Gilles spotted us and waved briefly, his hands full of cable.

Annick walked in with Gaëlle, both carrying crash helmets, and we went through the routine of kissing: "*Salut, salut...*"

By dusk the candles were lit, the place was crowded and we had to wait ages for our refills of cider.

Then Gilles appeared on the small stage. He'd put on an embroidered black waistcoat and a flat black hat. I hardly recognized him. He bowed, the lead from his guitar still trailing round his feet.

"*Bonsoir, mesdames, messieurs...*" We joined in the round of applause. Smoke hung in the air and candlelight flickered over that gaunt face, turning him into a figure from a Toulouse-Lautrec poster. His long dark hair had been slicked back for the performance and tied in a pigtail, and a heavy ring flashed as his fingers moved skilfully over the strings of the guitar.

He introduced each song in words I couldn't begin to make out.

"Too fast for us," said Amy.

"Not French," explained Angus. "Breton."

The songs were beautiful, strange, melancholy and sometimes funny because everyone laughed except us. Someone called out: "*Bretagne Libre!*" and people clapped and stamped.

"*La révolution commence a St Michel Chef-Chef,*" remarked Gaëlle cynically.

"Gilles is serious," protested Annick.

"No, he isn't," said Angus. "And this is the Vendée, not St Malo; they just like to pretend. Anyway, it wouldn't work. Brittany couldn't be self-sufficient."

"*Artichauts?*" joked Edouard, and we all laughed.

"But not much else," said Angus.

"We could trade." Edouard grinned at Amy and me. "Like the English, who grow nothing."

"Not true," I said. "Racist!"

Amy climbed up on her chair. "*Vive la Bretagne,*" she shouted and Gilles lifted a clenched fist.

"Turning into a terrorist?" teased Angus as she sat down.

But Amy looked thoughtful. "Now that would be an interesting role."

Hannah started nagging me for a grenadine.

"Oh God, Hannah," I said. "It costs a bomb!"

"Don't worry," said Gaëlle, fingering her intricately braided hair. "We pay. Then you pay for us when we come to your country."

When the performance was over, Gilles came down and joined us. "*Bravo*," he said, putting his arm round Amy.

"*Bravo, Gilles*," we all murmured and stood him a cider.

"*Viens chez nous*," invited Angus. "*Ils sont tous partis*."

"Not for much longer," I said hopefully.

"From Nantes?" Angus grinned. "You've forgotten how far it is."

Gilles looked at Amy. "You help me with the speakers?" Annick looked miffed.

"I could help too," said Hannah, picking up one of the cables.

"OK, why not? But do as I say, *la petite*, or . . ." and he drew his finger over his throat.

"*Attention, alors*," warned Annick, blowing him a kiss.

"We'll wait then," said Angus.

"Not necessary." Gilles smiled. "The two girls come with me in my big Mercedes Benz."

Annick groaned. "He mean his *vieux Renault Camper*."

Gilles pulled a face. "We follow you. OK?"

"I think Hannah ought to come with us," I said. After all, she was my responsibility.

"Oh, stop fussing Ellie," said Hannah. "You're as bad as Mum."

I felt relieved when the three of them eventually turned up at the house, Amy a little too close to Gilles and Hannah clinging adoringly to his hand.

Angus brought out some fresh cans of beer.

"*Quelle merveilleuse maison*," said Gilles, removing his hat and aiming it so that it landed on top of a big copper pan.

"*En anglais*," insisted Angus.

Gilles concentrated. "What a wonderful house. I can visit only when Angus is here. It is so sad."

We clapped and shouted "*Bravo!*"

"The name's a bit off." Amy snapped open a can and sat down close to Gilles. "I mean, Ellie keeps hearing wolves."

That made me mad. "Well, I'm not the only one."

Gilles looked baffled. "Wolves?"

"*Les loups de Chanteloup*," said Angus deprecatingly.

"Ah... And they hear them?"

"It's psychological," said Angus.

"Oh, come on," said Amy. "We're a lot saner than you!"

Outside, Annick and Gaëlle arrived with a roar. They came in – "*Salut...*" – unfastening their helmets. Gaëlle shook out her long plait, and Annick carefully arranged herself close to Gilles, her plump thighs bronze against her black lycra shorts.

Gilles slid his arms round Amy and Annick.

"*J'ai deux jolies filles. Quelle chance.*"

Amy stiffened and pulled away. "You haven't got this one," she said tartly.

Michel quickly changed the subject. "Once, you

know, no one come here, no one work here except the Augustes. She scare people, your old lady."

"Henriette? I thought she was rather sweet," I said.

"What about that wolf howl?" Amy reminded me.

"She's just a bit senile."

Gilles took out cigarette papers and a small metal box. "*On fume?*"

Angus frowned. "*Pas ici,*" he said sternly. "*Pas chez nous.*"

Gilles put the stuff away instantly. "*Comme tu veux . . .*" He looked miffed. "My grandmother say Henriette sleep with the Germans."

Annick sucked the back of her little finger: "*Oh, ta grandmère!*"

Gilles shrugged. "Old people remember."

"They tell stories."

"All stories have a little truth," said Gilles. He took out his guitar and began plucking the strings. "You know, this is the country of *Barbe Bleue.*"

"What's that?" asked Hannah.

"Bluebeard," said Angus.

Hannah yawned. "Is that the one with all those locked rooms? He's just a story."

"He was real," said Gilles. "There are songs . . ." He struck a chord. "People remember even now." His voice fell. "I am named for him – Gilles de Rais."

Angus looked irritated. "Oh, come off it, Gilles. You'll scare the kid silly."

Hannah was furious. "I am *not* a kid. And I'm *not* scared."

Gilles grinned at her. "We go to his castle, yes?"

"Yes, please!"

"Which one?" asked Angus. "He had dozens."

"*Machecoul, bien sûr*. It's very pretty. An old town."

"Gilles like the *fantômes*," explained Gaëlle scornfully. "His music . . . he collect ancient songs. And they make him a little. . ." She tapped her forehead with her finger.

"There are things we do not understand," said Gilles mysteriously.

"We will one day," said Angus. "It's just that people like fooling themselves."

"Not every time," said Annick. "You remember last year? That Ouija board?"

"What's a weejie board?" asked Hannah sleepily.

"We did that ourselves," argued Angus. "We subconsciously wanted it to spell out a name."

"You have it still?"

"I suppose so."

"In that cupboard," said Gilles. "It was there the last time. You permit?"

Angus sighed. "If you have to."

Gilles rummaged and brought out a circular board. "*Le voilà!*"

"Is it a kind of a game?" asked Hannah.

"That's right."

She peered at it. "Looks very boring," she said. "I'm going to bed."

Gaëlle was curious. "We do it, yes?"

"How do you play?" I asked.

"Don't you know?" said Amy. "You put a glass

128

upside down in the middle and we each put a finger on it."

"Why?"

"You ask it questions, dope. That's what the letters are for. I've got an aunty in Ireland who does it."

We heard a car pulling up outside.

"Too late," said Angus. "They're back."

A man's voice called out, "*Bonsoir. Bonne nuit. À bientôt . . .*" Then we heard Mum and Martine squawking in the hall like a couple of chickens on speed. They came bouncing into the kitchen all flushed and fluttery. Mum gave me a guilty look. "Nice evening?"

"Super," I said coolly. "How about yours?"

"Amusing. Hannah in bed?"

I nodded.

Martine pointed at the empty beer cans. "You lot had better stay the night," she said. "I don't want any accidents."

"But we are OK," protested Annick.

"Or fines." They looked incomprehending, not knowing the English word. "*Des amendes,*" she translated, and they nodded and groaned. "*Peut-être . . .*"

Then she spotted the Ouija board. "What a bunch of ghouls," she remarked, but I noticed her eyes going shifty again. "So what did the spirits have to tell you tonight?"

"Nothing," said Angus. "We haven't started yet."

"Well don't. It's not good to fool with things like that."

"Oh, Mum," sighed Angus. "Go to bed!"

We got a glass from the kitchen and placed our quivering fingers on its stem.

"French or English" whispered Michel. Annick began to giggle. "Stop. You're moving the glass."

"What shall we ask it?"

"Is there someone there?" declaimed Amy in her best theatrical voice.

The glass began to slide.

"You're pushing."

"No I'm not."

"It isn't picking out any letters."

Worlds meshing. I thought "Alain..." I called silently.

"*Espirit, que veus tu?*" intoned Giles.

The glass paused at an "E", then moved away. Many of the letters were scratched and indistinct. "It can't read them," said Amy.

"'L'," said Edouard. "Look."

The glass looped and returned.

"*Deux 'L',*" said Giles. "ELLE. Ah. It is a woman."

The glass slid again.

"*Look at that,*" said Amy. "*It's a 'Y'. E-L-L-Y. Elly. Ellie?* "She pointed at me. "*It wants her.*"

CHAPTER THIRTEEN

Martine had set a stew in a very low oven. By late morning, the kitchen was filled with the warm fragrance of meat, wine and herbs, and even that did nothing to lift my mood. All night long I'd been asking: had I really been called by some wandering spirit? Ellie... Ellie...

Or had Amy fixed it?

And that voice in the garden – Ellie... Ellie... Amy too? Why bother? Perhaps she was teasing, pushing me to see how far things would go. Maybe she thought I believed my own fantasy. Maybe I should talk tough to her. Amy wasn't dumb. She knew about imagination. She knew what I was like. And if I chose to nurture a crush on a photograph, that was my business, not hers.

I sat there, absorbing my morning fix of caffeine – oh screw Amy! I thought. Little ghost sounds came drifting in from the garden – a dog barking, a man grunting, a child's high voice burbling on. I heard the faint beat-beat of a drum and a fiddle, a baby crying, someone singing out of tune and a phrase of cool jazz picked out on a piano. Past? Present? They seemed to be all mixed up.

And inside the golden rectangle framed by the door three lacewings were dancing, moving round each other in complex loops. Time, I thought. Circular. No beginning, no end. Maybe in some way everything was now, and nothing ever really died.

Like love. You could go back along the loop and there it would be, Mum, Steve, baby Hannah and me. Happy families ... not that we really were. They argued. They fought. They tore each other apart. And I wanted them both.

I snapped out of it, picking up the scribbled note that our guests had left: *Merci pour tout. Edouard, Annick, Michel et Gaëlle.* Not Gilles, I noticed — he must have taken himself home. I walked boldly out into the bright day. Jules was barking at Amy and Hannah fooling about. I joined in the romp and my phantoms dissolved.

At half past one Martine appeared on the terrace banging on a big brass gong. "*À table!*"

We assembled dutifully in the dining-room. The table was covered with a starched white cloth and laid with napkins in silver rings and heavy ornate cutlery.

"So who's coming to lunch?" teased Angus.

"Us," said Martine. "It's Sunday." And she sang: "*I've treacle and toffee, I've teas and I've coffee, Soft tommy and succulent chops...*"

"*I've chickens and conies,*" warbled Mum, "*And*

pretty polonies, And excellent peppermint drops!"

And we all dutifully clapped. Well, the ladies expected it.

The meal should have been great, but we spoilt it by bickering.

Mum had made a starter of tuna fish salad, and Martine had brought out a glazed and scalloped tart which she'd put on the sideboard next to the fruit bowl. "*Bon appétit!*" she said optimistically, plopping a cork out of a bottle.

"Can I have some this time?" pleaded Hannah.

Martine conferred with Mum. "A little." She got up and drew in the shutters to break the sun dazzle which shimmered on the cloth and glittered in the cutlery and polished glasses. A couple of large bumble-bees drifted in through the gap.

Amy ducked. "Hornets!" she squealed. "Someone get rid of them."

"Honey-bees," corrected Angus. "If you don't flap and fuss they won't hurt you."

"I do not flap and fuss," said Amy icily. "I leave that sort of thing to Ellie."

I stiffened.

"Amy," said Mum. "Was that supposed to be funny?"

"Not really, no." Amy looked baffled. "I don't know why I said it."

"But Ellie *is* a fusspot," said Hannah. "You're right."

We concentrated on food, trying hard not to wreck that marvellous stew with indigestible words.

"Cheese," announced Martine.

Hannah sighed. "I'm full. Why do French people eat so much?'

"Why do English girls have to be so rude?" asked Mum.

"That's not rude," I said irritably. "She's only saying what she thinks."

Angus the peacemaker showed Hannah the fruit tart. "You've got room for some of this, haven't you?" Then he added his drop of verbal poison. "Pity it's apple."

Martine looked narked. "What would you have preferred, monsieur?"

"Something more typical."

"Like frogs' legs," said Amy with relish. "Drenched in that blackcurrant stuff Madame Auguste knocks back."

"You're disgusting," I said.

"No, I'm not. I'm just using my imagination. Like you."

"We should have got pears and almonds," said Angus, ignoring us.

"That's *provençale*," said Martine. "I wanted something local." She served the last slice. "And this has Calvados."

"They wouldn't know the difference." Angus realized what he'd just said. "I didn't mean..."

But Amy had picked it up.

"You," she announced delightedly, "are a French chauvinist pig."

Mum shook her head. "Why are we all so bad-tempered?"

By the time Martine brought in the coffee, the atmosphere had become explosive. She filled five cups, then sat down heavily. "Chrissie and I are knackered," she said. "You lot can do the washing-up."

Mum brought out the obligatory cigarette.

I said, "Do you have to?" but she bit back at me, "Yes I do."

Hannah got up. "I'm going out to talk to Margot."

"Why not?" Through a veil of cancerous smoke, Mum smiled wanly. "You'll get a pleasanter conversation out of a donkey than out of any of us."

"Why d'you think I'm going?"

"Maybe we should take a siesta," said Martine. "It's too hot. That's what's wrong."

The three of us cleared the table. We didn't trust ourselves to talk much. Washing up seemed endless.

"Did anyone else get a message from that Ouija board?" I enquired cynically.

"Not really," said Angus. "We gave up on it soon after you left." He stacked the last plate, then went off upstairs.

"You shouldn't have gone," said Amy. "It needed you as a focus."

"Don't be stupid," I said, trying not to feel flattered.

We slung the soggy tea cloths over bushes to dry.

"Let's go," said Amy.

"Go where?"

"Over to those woods again. We could row across to that island — it'd be cool there." She slipped her arm through mine as we walked round to the front and over the lawn. "How does it feel to be called by a spirit?"

I moved away instantly. "I don't actually believe in spirits," I said. "But I do believe in people who fake things."

Amy looked offended. "The glass moved. I felt it. I didn't fake anything."

"Well, somebody did."

"Well, it wasn't me."

The woods were shady and resinous and riddled with rabbit tracks. It was hard for me to believe it was the same place I'd battled through the other night. Amy pointed out a dark burrow ringed with brush. "Bet that's where your wolf lives," and she shook her hair wild and called out, "*Awooo!*"

"*Awooo!*" I yelled back. After the tense atmosphere of lunch it was such a relief to fool around.

Down at the water's edge, gossamer threads from the overhanging willow dangled miniature caterpillars over our heads. Amy looked up and shrieked. "There's one in my hair!"

I picked it out for her. "So who doesn't flap and fuss?"

A little way off shore, the boat was bobbing free.

"We forgot to tie it," said Amy. She looked at me meaningfully. "One of us will have to go out and fetch it."

I gazed across at the island, at its sun-smudged greens and browns and its dark hem fringed with reeds. A couple of geese landed in front of it, cutting a swathe through the water, then bobbing about like bath toys. It seemed ordinary now, even jolly – like an island in the middle of a boating lake. What a place to spend a lazy afternoon, I thought.

Amy sighed. "I'll do it." She stripped to her knickers and swam out to the boat, made a grab: "Got you!" and clambered aboard. The boat swayed and righted itself.

Suddenly I heard it. A voice. Calling me. "Ellie. Ellie . . ."

I froze.

"Someone wants you," shouted Amy. "You deaf or something?"

So she'd heard it too. I relaxed. "I know," I said. "I'll go and check."

"Well, don't be long," said Amy. "This boat leaves in five minutes – OK?"

Halfway across the meadow I met Martine, wading through the heat with a big bunch of flowers she'd evidently just picked.

"Where were you?" she asked.

"By the lake. With Amy."

"Have you checked that boat?"

"We've already been out in it," I told her smugly.

"Well, do be careful." She toed the dry grass with the tip of her sandal. She seemed suddenly awkward, self-conscious, her usual flamboyance all fizzled out. "I thought you might like a small outing," she said.

Something was up, I thought. "To where?" I asked suspiciously.

"St Yves." She smiled. "You've seen him already – our bishop with the woodworm."

I nodded, puzzled. "Is it a place as well?"

"Of course."

"To do what?"

Martine shrugged. "Chrissie told me you liked old graveyards." (Yes I did, but so what?) "I'm going to take flowers to my parents' grave. I always do when we come over."

"Isn't Angus going with you?"

"He doesn't like to."

"So what about Mum?"

Martine looked embarrassed. "I thought you and I might have a talk."

Oh yes, I thought. Clever stuff (bet that was Mum's idea). They wanted me to face up to reality, see his name on a tombstone, Alain...

Alain what? I wondered.

"What was your French name?" I asked innocently. "Before you got married?"

Martine looked baffled. "De Guillaumet."

Alain de Guillaumet. It sounded like music. I wanted to see it written down, even on a tombstone. "OK, I'll come," I said. "But I'll have to tell Amy."

I walked back to the lake and found the boat drifting halfway across, its oars gently buffeted by the water.

"Amy?" I called anxiously.

She sat up in the boat.

"I'm going out with Martine."

"Please yourself," she called, paddling one hand in the water. "See you later."

I walked back to the house. Martine was waiting. We got into the Volvo. It felt odd strapping myself into the front seat.

I didn't know what to say, so I said nothing and just stared out of the window, concentrating on the scenery.

We passed a little run-down château with a fairy-tale roof, standing in a moat yellow with chickweed. We passed a couple of shrines with dead flowers and statues, two or three signs for a big supermarket and an out-of-date poster for a long-forgotten disco. Then we drove in and out of a village. I read its name – St Yves.

"Why do we have their bishop?" It was the first thing I'd said since we'd left the house.

"He was a pious object." We parked outside a walled enclosure at the top of a small hill. "People prayed to him. And to Sainte Anne – you've seen our Sainte Anne, haven't you?" We walked in through the big iron gates. "Sainte Anne could find you a lover," she said. "Or even give you a child if you couldn't conceive."

I was amused. "Did people really believe that crap?"

"People still do." Martine turned and looked at me. "You are not so different."

Ah. That was it, I told myself: the beginning of the lecture.

I followed her dumbly through the streets of the dead, between monuments, angels and miniature chapels. I lingered over plastic posies and framed photographs of the dear departed, putting off my response.

"What was that supposed to mean?" I challenged at last.

She took a small iron key out of her bag and unlocked the door of one of the chapels. The place was about the same size as a big garden shed, but it had a couple of pews, an altar with a tarnished crucifix, and two tiny church windows, their stained glass looped with cobwebs.

Martine whipped off the lace altar cloth and shook out dust, dried petals and a mass of dead flies. "People believe what they need to believe." She was breathless with effort. "Sometimes it's easier to fancy a ghost than a real person. And you won't find him there, Ellie." (She'd spotted me reading the memorial plaques in the wall.)

"Why not?" I asked, instantly betraying myself.

She filled two dented metal pots with water from a standpipe and pushed in the flowers, stem by stem.

"Because this is supposed to be holy ground. They wouldn't accept a suicide."

I was shocked. "What's unholy about suicide?"

"It's a form of murder."

"You can't murder yourself!" I felt furious. "Didn't his family make a fuss?"

"His family tried to hush things up." She took a small Thermos out of her shoulder bag. "Coffee?"

I nodded, surprised. It seemed a bit off to be doing the picnic thing there.

We sat astride the pew. There was just room for the two of us.

"That's so unkind," I said at last. "He must have been desperately unhappy."

Martine shrugged. "Some say he made his own unhappiness. And other people's."

140

"What d'you mean?"

She broke off two squares of chocolate and offered me one. "Alain's very seductive, isn't he?"

I closed up like a clam. "I wouldn't know."

"I would." She poured out more coffee. "I stayed at Chanteloup one summer. I must have been, maybe, fifteen, sixteen. There were several of us, all young. Cousins." She screwed the top on the Thermos and put it away. "I felt it then. Something insidious, disturbing, attractive, but somehow controlled because Henriette ruled the place like an iron lady. People were scared of Henriette. We were scared of her, but I was more scared of something else..." She laughed. "Maybe sex. Then one of the cousins died. A young girl. Drowned in the lake where they found Alain. An accident, they said, but people talk, and people have long memories in places like this. Even after Henriette was sent to the Home, another girl drowned." Martine sighed. "Coincidence, of course. She was trespassing. After nuts, I think – what a price to pay. Tried to swim to the island."

I shivered. "They found him there? In the lake?"

Martine looked puzzled. "I thought I told you," she said. "In the car the other day. When we were both being so unpleasant..." She suddenly leaned forward and gave me a hug. "I put up all those KEEP OUT signals, but you just wouldn't shut up."

I felt ashamed. "I'm really sorry."

"You had no choice, I think." We closed up the chapel and walked back to the car. "I am not superstitious, Ellie." She started the engine. "I am a dentist, not a ghost hunter. But keep off nonsense like that old Ouija board. I don't believe in ghosts, but bad vibes make their own ghosts and I don't want your holiday spoilt."

"It's not being," I said and I meant it. "And I'm not obsessed, honestly – just curious." That was fast becoming my motto.

"And you wouldn't like to change your room?"

"It's not worth it," I said stubbornly. "I'm OK."

"That Ouija board," Martine said thoughtfully. "Bet it was Gilles's idea."

I grinned. "Yes it was."

Martine sighed. "Gilles hasn't been round here for long and already he has too much influence. Angus's friends, the people he grew up with, they are not the same any more. Gilles is older, and talented; he's made one or two records and that impresses. He's a good musician, but he takes his research far too seriously."

So what? I thought. He's attractive. He's cool.

Back at the house we found Angus and Hannah playing tiddly-winks on the terrace and Mum stretched out, reading and smoking, between the lengthening shadows on the lawn.

"I'll go and find Amy," I said. I climbed into the meadow and ran through the wood.

"I'm back!" I called, but there was no reply.

Then I noticed the boat-shell bobbing empty on the water.

Coincidence?

Two girls dead. Wasn't three a magic number?

I screamed out: "Amy!"

On the island a bushy head rose out of the foliage.

"Hi!" shouted Amy. "Come and see what I've found."

CHAPTER
FOURTEEN

Amy got into the boat and rowed over to pick me up. "What's the panic?" she said, pulling in to the shore.

I climbed aboard. "What panic?"

"The way you yelled out my name, I thought the wolf must be after you."

I lay back, combing my fingers through the glassy depths that had once been Alain's shroud. The island loomed close, catching us in its net of shadows. The boat see-sawed wildly as we got out. I stepped apprehensively, half anticipating some unknown terror, but the pebbles were just pebbles and the grass was just grass and I had to duck sideways to avoid a dragonfly.

I watched Amy tethering the boat to a stump. "So what have you found?"

"Just wait and see," she said tantalizingly.

So I waited and saw – polished ivy leaves winding round lichened hawthorns, sunlight lying scooped inside the hollows of kingcups, and fading azalea blossoms, all peaches and cream, fluttering like rags through the brambles and gorse. I sighed. A dream island...

Amy clambered over a rock. "Come on."

I followed her dumbly.

"Where did you go?" she called back.

"To a churchyard."

She turned round and gaped at me. "To do what?"

"Martine was putting flowers on her parents' grave."

Amy looked incredulous. "Why did she need you?"

"She thought I might be interested."

Amy sighed. "You're a ghoul, Eleanor Portman and everyone knows it."

I acted the part, intoning, "Ooohoo" and flapping my arms about. Then I asked her again. "So what have you found?"

She smirked. "Something right up your street."

"What d'you mean?"

"Come and see."

In the middle of the island a stunted palm and a couple of undersized pines rose incongruously out of a tangle of shrubs. Amy squatted beside a boulder. "Here." She parted leggy fronds of rosemary. "Look at this..."

I drew a breath. Inexpertly carved was the name I had longed to see:

ALAIN DE GUILLAUMET
MORT 1933

Suddenly the whole island seemed to vibrate with his presence.

From somewhere else I could hear Amy's voice: "That the guy in your room?"

I nodded, running my fingers over the letters. Then I turned to her. "How did you find it?"

She looked sheepish.

"I was exploring the place, then I needed to pee. I squatted down behind those bushes..." she pointed. "Then I saw what looked like a letter carved into that rock, so when I finished I came over..." She hesitated. "Funny — finding it made me feel really odd — sort of shivery, excited." She looked at me. "Is that how he affects you?"

"He doesn't *affect* me at all."

Amy raked back her hair. "So he's buried out here. I wonder why?"

"Because," I said stiffly, "he had the misfortune to kill himself."

"Oh, yes of course," said Amy. "They couldn't have put him in the churchyard. Suicide's a sin."

I was amazed. "How would you know?"

"I'm a Catholic, you know that."

"Well, I think that attitude's rotten," I said. "It's his family that gets hurt."

"Maybe he hurt his family," said Amy stubbornly.

"How?" I demanded. "By being desperate? Why didn't they help him?"

Amy was silent.

At last she said, "You're right, Ellie. It's just my dad. He's religious. And we were taught all that crap at Sunday school."

"You should have my dad," I joked. "He'd discuss suicide as an art form."

"Aren't you lucky?" said Amy. It wasn't my idea of luck.

"I suppose she knows it's here," I mused.

"Who knows what's here?"

"The gravestone. Martine."

"How would she? After all, Alain was years ago. Before World War Two even."

I remembered our conversation. "She's more involved than you might think."

"So what?" said Amy. "It's her family." She broke off a stem of rock rose and propped it against the stone. "Look. A flower for your Alain."

I felt an instant pang of jealousy. He was my fantasy, not hers. Amy had Angus and Gilles. Even sober Edouard had flicked a lustful glance in her direction. And now Alain . . .

"Aren't you a romantic?" I remarked coldly.

Amy smirked. "Look who's talking." She moved away. "Coming?"

I followed her down to the shore where she'd left her beach towel. She flopped on to it, patting the space beside her: "Be my guest . . ." and popped a sweet into her mouth. "Have one," she offered. Her breath smelt of aniseed.

I arranged myself awkwardly, arms about knees, the strongly-flavoured sweet jiggling over my tongue. A goose sailed inshore, eyeing us with interest. Then it struggled up the bank and waddled across, making small triangular prints on the smooth stones.

Amy giggled and held out an aniseed ball. "You wouldn't like one of these . . ." The goose extended its neck, snapped at the sweet, then dropped it with a hiss. "Don't blame me," she called after it as it waddled crossly back to the water. "I did warn you."

Then she yawned and turned to me. "What do you think of Gilles?"

"I don't," I said, irritated by her change of mood.

"Martine doesn't like him."

"How do you know?"

"It's obvious."

"Well, Hannah does."

"Oh, Hannah," Amy sighed. "Listen. This holiday," she said. "Know what it's like?"

I didn't care, but she told me anyway.

"Theatre. That incredible house − it's like a backdrop." She rolled on to her stomach so that her profile vanished inside a tangle of hair. "And we've all taken on roles. It's not just me. Haven't you noticed?"

"So who's writing the script?" I asked tartly.

"That's just what I'd like to know." She turned to face me. "Wouldn't you?"

I avoided that question.

"I'm not playing a role."

Amy laughed. "You should step outside your skin and watch yourself, Ellie Portman. Even Hannah's overacting."

"Hannah always overacts."

"And look at your mum and Guy."

I flicked a small iridescent beetle off my leg. "I'd rather not," I said.

"Did Martine arrange that, I wonder?" blundered Amy. "He's so good for your mum. Keeps saying nice things to her."

"It's just a holiday flirtation."

"Not even that. Oh, Ellie, you're so possessive."

"I lost my dad," I burst out. "I can't afford to lose Mum."

"You haven't lost your dad," argued Amy. "You get to see him lots. I used to come with you."

When we were still kids, I thought, but now things had changed. He was a flirt. Didn't mean a thing, but I couldn't stand him looking at Amy. Not in that way (or had I just imagined it?).

"I embarrass him," I said. "Make him feel old."

"Oh, Ellie, he's your dad. He loves you."

I sighed. "Steve's too busy trying to find himself to love anyone. Anyway, he prefers Hannah."

"Oh, Ellie."

"Wish I had a dad like yours," I said. "Normal."

"Your dad's even more normal. Listen I've caught my old man ogling girls when he thought we weren't looking. It's just a game with them."

"Well, mine plays it for real."

"Well, yours had the opportunity, didn't he? All those students and then that book – he was like a guru for a while, remember? Listen, I couldn't guarantee how mine would behave if he got to be rich and famous."

"Dad's not famous," I protested. "And he'll be on Income Support if the Institute chucks him out."

Amy took another sweet. "What was it like, that book?"

"I showed it to you."

"That was years ago. I was a kid."

"Oh, you know. Stories with some kind of a

149

hidden message; critics called it Zen. Psychological stuff ... bits about meditation, how to develop your creativity..."

"Leave your wife," crowed Amy. "Screw around."

"Oh, he's not that bad," I said defensively. "Just a bit immature."

Amy giggled. "So, look who's talking."

We lazed for a while, watching dragonflies and water boatmen skimming the surface of the lake. Then we untied the boat and rowed back. The sun was quite low by then and the midges were hunting in packs, hovering like dust mites in the golden air. We slashed out at them but they kept regrouping.

I suddenly found I was feeling good.

I knew what it was.

"We haven't talked properly for ages, you and me."

"You kept putting up barriers," said Amy.

"What about you? You can't have a conversation with a sexpot."

"Who says so?"

"Dunno," I said feebly. I grinned. "Wasn't me."

We tied up the boat and wandered back to the house.

On the lawn Angus was doing handstands, showing off to Hannah, while Jules leapt about, barking furiously.

Martine looked up from her drink. "Nice afternoon?"

"Great," said Amy. "We've been on that island." She looked at me questioningly, but I shook my head.

Martine swirled the remains of her drink. "Why don't we go to the beach?" she said. "And watch the sun go down."

"Sounds good," said Mum, stubbing out her cigarette.

So we took ourselves off to St Michel, culled the last of the doughnuts from the *beignet* man and sat munching them, wiggling our toes in the cooling sand.

"We've been planning a barbecue," announced Angus. "On the beach at St Brevin. It was Gilles's idea – a sort of farewell party for *les anglais*. What do you think?"

"Sounds wild," said Amy.

"Who's paying?" asked Martine.

"We can all muck in."

"And how do you propose to get home afterwards?"

"That's where you come in."

"Oh great," said Martine. "Chrissie and I stay up half the night and then ferry you lot back in the small hours?"

"I didn't mean that," said Angus. "You'd be invited. Edouard's lot and Michel's too – a big family get-together. We could even ask Guy. And Marie-Luce and Cathérine. Everyone. The Augustes..."

Martine burst out laughing. "I can just see Madame," she said, "sitting on a beach, eating a sausage!"

"And disco dancing." Amy got up and began shimmying about.

"Gaëlle's aunt might come, and Annick's brother."

"The one with the van?"

Angus nodded.

"Convenient," said Martine, "if he stays with the orange juice."

"I'll stay with the grenadine," offered Hannah.

"That's no good," teased Amy. "You can't drive."

"I could learn. Angus could teach me."

"Anyway," I added, "who says you're invited?"

Hannah climbed over Angus and pulled at his ears. "I'm coming. You tell them."

Angus swung her in the air and bounced her down. "We couldn't have it without you." He looked sideways at Martine. "It's on then?"

"We'll think about it," said Martine regally.

We went for a stroll along the water's edge.

I said casually to Angus, "Do you know where your great uncle What's-it is buried?"

"Alain?"

I nodded. "He's not in that chapel place where I went with your mum."

"He committed suicide," said Angus. "Mum must have told you. They wouldn't have him up there."

"Oooh the meanies," exclaimed Hannah, not understanding a word.

Amy barged in with her usual subtlety. "So where did they put him then? In with the artichokes?"

"Oh, Amy," reprimanded Mum.

"Something like that," Martine said quietly.

I felt awful. I hadn't meant Martine to hear. I hadn't meant to hurt her feelings.

"How dreadful," said Mum, brushing sugar crystals from around her mouth. "Why did they have to be so harsh?"

"It's a sin," explained Amy. "Taking human life. Like abortion."

"That's not a sin," said Mum.

"Depends on your point of view," said Martine.

Mum turned to Amy. "So you wouldn't? Even if you were raped?"

"I don't know," said Amy, cornered, "do I?"

"And what about war?" Mum went on relentlessly. "That's taking life. Do they think war's OK?"

"Religion," growled Angus. "Hypocritical..."

"Not all religion," I said. "Quakers aren't like that."

Mum sighed. "It would be nice if some of the pleasant bits were true. We all need a bit of magic sometimes."

"Magic *is* true," said Hannah stoutly.

"Of course it is," said Angus. "Gilles believes in it."

"Gilles would," said Martine. She pointed. "That's magic – look!" Beyond us the ocean lay pleated with gold, its horizon veiled in a rosy mist. She sighed. "Can't you just see some drowned city rising out of those waves? Montoise."

After supper I went to my room, undressed, and relit the candle in the crimson pot.

Then, roosting in the feathered hollow at the end of my unmade bed, I communed again with that face I had come to love. I thought of the letters carved into stone: ALAIN DE GUILLAUMET. So the churchyard wouldn't have him? Alain wouldn't have cared.

I smiled, seeing some jowly, self-satisfied priest with his nose turned up: "A suicide? Not on my patch. Only respectable bodies in here."

But why had he killed himself?

There just had to be a woman, I thought as I fluffed up the mattress and smoothed down the sheets. Some friend of his sister's who'd turned him down. I remembered the image of Henriette in that droopy white dress, pale headband over cropped hair and dark teasing eyes. Mixed doubles? Maybe somewhere there was a girl we would never see, some role-playing sexpot like Amy.

I would never have rejected Alain.

I adjusted the shutters and snuggled back into that puffball of a bed. He'd died of a broken heart, I decided, as I lay awake, listening to the owls. And that lake had been his coffin. I could see him lying in its depths like Snow White in her glass box, gazing up at the sky through sightless eyes, his hair spread like water weed...

I shivered and quickly brought him back to life.

He was sitting for his portrait.

That portrait...

I built up the scene. I knew a bit about photography, had even joined the school club.

We'd need a white sheet pinned up as a backdrop. Lighting might be difficult with no proper spots, but there was always sunshine. I arranged him fussily in one of those curly chairs from the library. He sat, aimiable, tolerant, grumbling mildly: "*Tu sais? J'ai du travail a faire...*"

Outside the wolf began to sing.

"*Oohooo*," I warbled flippantly and pulled the sheet over my head.

The sun had moved round. The lighting was perfect.

My brother Paul slid a plate into the camera.

"Now?" I questioned and he nodded. "*Oui.*"

"Hold it," I said and I took the shot...

CHAPTER FIFTEEN

I finally took over that cavernous bathroom on the second floor. Showers were all very well, but I needed a soak.

The cistern gluggled and shuddered, and water dribbled into the big iron tub in a thin sinewy stream. I poured in some bubblebath and settled down for a long wait.

Someone rattled at the door, then muttered, "*Merde!*"

"I'm running a bath," I yelled.

"I know," grumbled Angus. "That means you'll be in there all morning."

"Too bad," I said triumphantly. "You should have got up earlier."

I sat, watching the milk-veined puddle creeping at a snail's pace up the sides of the tub. I could see what Angus meant. I should have brought in a book.

Below in the garden I could hear voices. I pushed up the window and stuck my head through a gap in the Virginia creeper. "Hi!"

Mum and Hannah looked up in astonishment, seeing my disembodied head growing out of the leaves. Then Mum grinned. "Rapunzel!" she called.

Obligingly I shook out my rats' tails.

"Not long enough," yelled Hannah. "So you don't get the prince!"

I stuck out my tongue. "Don't want him, so there."

When the bath was just over a third full, I gave up and stepped into it, arranging myself awkwardly on its funny moulded seat. The bubbles had flattened into cloudy swirls, out of which my knees rose like two pink eggs. I ran my fingers through them, making curly smoke patterns. *Alain*... I doodled, and the questions flooded in.

Had the island been his? Was he really buried there? Had the stone marked a grave? Or was it just a memorial?

And who had carved the letters?

Not me, said the stonemason. Wouldn't touch the job. He's a suicide. Brings bad luck.

I grinned at my fantasy – stories again. In a way, I supposed, Amy was right – this holiday *was* theatrical and we were all overacting. Amy the sexpot provoking Angus, Mum making up to a Frenchman, Martine going on about her mysterious past and me in love with a ghost. Not to mention Hannah. Holidays transform people, Steve used to say. I wouldn't have known; we never had that many.

Trying to immerse more of myself in that

157

lukewarm water, I lay back, looking up at the rust-spotted ceiling and those crumbling plaster walls marbled with birdshit. Then I washed and got out, standing dripping on the duckboard. The towels were thick like my gran's and rough from many washings. I pummelled myself pink, slipped into the bathrobe Mum had made me, and ran back upstairs to dress.

Through my open window came a shriek from Martine. "Not out here!" She sounded furious.

I looked down and saw Hannah, done up in a fringed silk scarf and her beloved donkey-bonnet, holding one of those old-fashioned dolls. "It's wax!" Martine was shouting. "Don't you understand?"

But poor Hannah looked baffled.

"The doll will melt in this heat."

"Ooh . . ." wailed Hannah, comprehending. She got up and followed Martine inside, protesting weepily: "Well how was I to know?"

I pulled on shorts and a top and went down for a coffee. In the kitchen I found Martine contrite, trying to cheer Hannah up. "You look so pretty in that shawl. I know – why don't we all dress up? Then we could go out and take some silly snaps."

"Not before breakfast," yawned Amy, busily burning toast.

Mum shook her head. "Amy, you're hopeless. You'll never get a husband."

"Don't particularly want one," said Amy, scraping off the charcoal. "And anyway, I don't need to cook – I'm a sexpot. Ellie said so."

Mum glanced at me, puzzled. "How would Ellie know?"

"Oh, Mum," I snapped.

"Children, children," chided Martine.

"Let's dress up," said Hannah, "like she said."

"*She's* the cat's mother," corrected Mum automatically.

"Dress up in what?" asked Amy.

"Anything you find, within reason. Just be careful."

Amy looked at me meaningfully. "That dress," she said.

"Oh, I couldn't!"

"Which one is that?" asked Martine.

"You'll see. . ."

Upstairs in her room Amy took it out and laid it on the bed.

"I can't," I protested. "She meant dress-up clothes, not something as special as this."

"Oh, Martine won't mind," said Amy. "It's only for a photograph."

I let her persuade me. It wasn't difficult. I took off my T-shirt and shorts and let her slip the dress over my head. The silk flowed over my flesh like cool, cool water. "Look at you!" said Amy admiringly. Then she frowned. "Your hair's all wrong."

She sat me down and began fussing, brushing it out and pinning it back. "It needs something else," and she rummaged in a drawer and found a silk scarf with fringes.

I was getting bored with being a model. "Listen," I said. "This is supposed to be a spoof, not a fashion show."

But Amy was off. "You need earrings really. Clip-ons and I haven't got any – Ellie, why don't you get your ears done? OK, let's try this." And she twisted the scarf and tied it round my hair. "That looks good," she said. She stuck out her tongue and put her head sideways. "You know, maybe you should get it cut. Suits you short. Come on – I'll do the war paint next."

When she'd finished she stood back to assess me.

"Oh, my God, Ellie!" She pointed. "Not trainers."

But I'd had enough. "How about you?" I said to distract her. "What are you going to put on?"

It worked. "Just wait and see."

I watched her riffling delicately through that over-stuffed wardrobe, pulling out a Cinderella-size pair of court shoes for me – "Try these" – and holding up a long Victorian nightgown spotted with blood or iron mould. She tried a man's quilted jacket, then a full peasant skirt ("miles too small," she groaned), then a tatty crimson caftan, sixties-style, with lots of gold braid and tassles.

Amy chose the caftan. "A bit hippie," she said, parading in front of me. "What d'you think?"

But I kept catching glimpses of myself in the mirror, a stranger, eyes blackened, the cheeks rouged and the mouth crayoned in that silly Cupid's bow. Amy'd looped back my hair so that it looked short, and tied the scarf low on my forehead so that when I moved, the fringes flickered.

I pulled a face, but the girl in the mirror simply

smiled and looked coy.

I froze in terror. "Amy, come here!"

"Can't," Amy mumbled. "I'm doing my mouth."

Down in the garden I could hear Martine singing and Hannah prattling away to Mum. I turned and saw Amy tweezing out a hair. Imagination again, I thought; watch it, Ellie.

Reassured, I looked back, but there *she* was. Her. Not me. Not Ellie. Smiling. Knowing.

"Amy!" I yelled.

"What's wrong now?" She came over and stepped between us. She'd put on a hat with an ostrich feather. "*Voilà!*" she sang, striking a pose.

I pushed her aside. "Look at me," I said, pointing at my own reflection.

But Amy wasn't impressed. "OK, OK, so you look amazing. So what?"

We've got some of those photos in the album. People gawp at them and say things like: "That one of your pantomimes?" There we all are – Martine in white drawstring bloomers too full even for her, Mum looking goggle-eyed in a frilly bonnet and a long apron, Angus in an embroidered dressing gown with a big gold sash, his arm round a glittering Amy whose hair cascades wildly over that crimson caftan. There's Hannah in her donkey hat and that silky shawl with the splashy flowers, holding a pair of sunglasses in front of a long-suffering Jules. And there am I in that dress, the princess whose feet were too big. . .

* * *

We each had a turn with the camera, even Hannah.

I was composing my shot when last night's dream came flooding back. That moment was eternity. Suddenly the light had always been gold, the tree shadows always that shape, and the lizard curled across my grey and white trainer would be poised there for centuries.

Circular. Time.

Nothing died.

I was vaguely aware of Amy getting at Angus, and Hannah yelling at Jules: "Come back, you horrible dog!" And from a long way away Mum's voice calling: "Come on Ettie!"

I jumped. "What did you call me?"

"Don't be all day."

That was what he'd said, smiling indulgently: "Don't take all day, Ettie."

And I knew what I'd say next, because I'd said it before. "Hold it!" I called and I took my shot.

A car moved slowly through the trees on the driveway. A door slammed and Guy came walking across the lawn, looking quite human in jeans and a sports shirt. Mum immediately ducked behind Amy. Even Martine looked a bit flustered. "*Pantomime*," she explained apologetically.

Guy walked up to me. "*Tu permets?*" He took the camera out of my frozen hands. "We must have you in this one. You look *très belle*." Then he pointed at my trainers and grinned. "*Sauf les baskets*."

So in that final shot there I am, standing rather

stiffly, anchored to the lawn by my enormous shoes, next to Angus who looks uneasy – that dress had unnerved him again...

"All change," yelled Martine. "Some of those clothes are delicate." She looked at me. "Especially that one."

I suddenly felt awful. "Did you mind?"

She touched my shoulder and smiled and I felt close to her again. "Not at all," she said. "As long as you're careful. It seems sad to put beautiful things away for ever."

"Who did it belong to? Do you know?"

She lifted a corner of the silk. "Bias cut. Thirties. Henriette perhaps, or maybe Nadine. They had some social life."

Mum was rushing away when I grabbed her. "You called me Ettie!"

She turned abstractedly. "Did I? When?"

"Ellie is the short name?" asked Guy.

"I'm Eleanor," I said, unwilling to be diverted, but Mum had already gone.

"A beautiful, medieval name. The name of queens. You are fortunate."

I smirked. What could I say? It was even getting to me, that charm.

I came down in shorts and a T-shirt to hear Angus going on about the barbecue. "Just two days before we go back to England," he was saying to Guy. "Will you come?"

Mum had fluffed out her hair and put on the flowery sundress she'd made for the holiday.

"Assuming it's happening," said Martine tartly.

"Oh, we're doing it anyway," said Angus airily.

"With you or without you."

"Oh, please come," said Amy persuasively. She'd changed into sober jeans and a spotted shirt. "It would be much more fun to have us all together."

"That's emotional blackmail, my girl." Martine frowned, calculating. "So. Mince for hamburgers and how many *merguez*? Spicy sausages to you lot."

Angus grinned. "Oh, thanks Mum."

"I should think so too. We can work it all out this evening." She turned to Guy. "*Un apéritif?* I'd ask you to lunch but we need to shop."

"For the barbecue?"

"For lunch."

"I have an idea," said Guy. "Why don't we make a little tour? Take the two cars over to Machecoule? By the time we get there, the *traiteurs* will be open and we can buy a picnic."

"Are you sure?" said Martine.

Guy winked at Mum. "Good for my English."

"Bad for your English," teased Mum, "if you listen to my lot."

I was diverted from my usual irritation (you can tell Mum's a teacher) by something niggling at the back of my mind, some jigsaw puzzle piece that I couldn't see, making a pattern that I couldn't understand.

And: "Hold it", I remembered saying as I took the shot.

We shared ourselves between the two cars. Amy and I got into the Volvo and watched Hannah pulling faces at us all from the back of Guy's

Citroën as we moved in convoy down the drive. Hold it...

"Do you ever get the feeling you've said or done something before?" I said to Amy. "I mean, in a dream or in some other life?"

"That's called a *déjà vu*," said Martine, overhearing.

"I know what you mean," Amy said. "It's creepy – as if everything was sort of pre-planned and you had no real choice."

I shivered. "Like you said – a script."

"That's right."

"There was an old religious argument," said Angus from the front seat, "about whether people ever had free will."

"Of course people have free will," said Amy.

"Parents programme you," declared Angus gloomily. "Just like computers."

"Oh, if only we could," murmured Martine.

"Speak for yourself," said Amy. "I'm not a computer."

"But sometimes people do seem to have no choice," said Martine. "They call that fate."

We skimmed through dappled lanes, looped round into flat, marshy country, pausing, flagged down by Guy, to admire wildfowl and yellow iris. Then we turned west towards the coast again.

Guy pulled into a lay-by. "Look up!" he called, and high on a hill we saw the grim ruins of a medieval castle.

"One of Bluebeard's places," Angus explained.

Hannah stuck her head out of the car in front.

"Gilles is going to take me there!" she shrieked, pointing.

"So what?" I yelled back.

"Wasn't Gilles named after that Bluebeard guy?" asked Amy.

Angus exploded. "Oh, don't be naive. Gilles is a perfectly ordinary name in France and his last name is Triquet, not de Rais."

"Triquet," I punned feebly. "Well, he's certainly that!"

We followed the Citroën down to Machecoule and parked beside it in the main square. The shops were beginning to wake up after their long noon siesta.

The town was ancient and quaint. We lingered in its narrow streets, bought postcards, drooled over shop windows, even visited the church.

Angus made the houses come alive for us. He wasn't showing off. He was just crazy about old buildings and he knew so much.

We chose our *traiteur* and for about twenty minutes stood squabbling amiably over what to buy.

Guy waved a note at the girl behind the counter.

"*Oh non, Guy!*" protested Martine.

"My pleasure," insisted Guy. "So. We picnic *chez Barbe Bleue*?"

"Why not?" said Mum.

We drove back the way we'd come and parked adjacent to the ruins.

"Now we climb," said Guy.

When we'd reached a sort of summit, we spread

our booty out on the grass.

"I'm starving," said Hannah.

"*Alors, mange toi,*" said Guy.

Hannah worked that one out. "*Oh, oui,*" she said, pleased with herself. She tucked into a wedge of quiche. "Was his beard really blue?"

"Oh, yes." Guy took a swig of mineral water. "Would you like me to tell you how it got that way?"

Hannah, loving stories, deserted her beloved Angus and moved closer to Guy. "Yes, please."

"One day, Gilles de Rais—"

"Was he Bluebeard?"

"Oh, yes. And he was riding through the forest when he met a beautiful lady and her brother who was a knight."

I was intrigued. I liked stories too.

"They had been attacked..." Guy drew his finger across his throat "by robbers, and the lady was weeping. So Gilles took them home to his castle."

"So he *was* nice," concluded Hannah.

"Ah," said Guy ominously. "But wait. Once inside, he put the brother into a dungeon. Then he found a priest and forced the lady to marry him."

"The rat," murmured Mum.

"But when the priest had said the words, the lady, whose name was Blanche, suddenly turned into a blue devil."

"Oh, goody," said Hannah.

"And she said, "I've had enough of your evil acts, Gilles de Rais, so from now on you shall wear my colour." And his beard, which had been red – " and he pointed at Angus's ginger stubble – "turned blue."

"Watch it Angus," joked Amy.

"And the devil took him down to the deepest pits of..." He struggled for the word. "*L'enfer?*"

"Hell!" we all shouted.

"*Merci.* And that's how his beard became blue." He took out a packet of cigarettes and offered one to Mum.

Martine frowned. "You should go down to the deepest pits of hell, Guy Lebrun."

Guy looked hurt. "*Mais pourquoi?*"

"You encourage my friend Chrissie to smoke."

"But she smokes already."

"Stop nannying me, Martine!" snapped Mum. She gazed all shiny-eyed at Guy, through fresh curls of smoke. "You're a great storyteller..." she began. Then she inhaled at the wrong moment and began to cough.

"You see?" said Martine.

Mum spluttered, then giggled, and we all laughed too. Guy wasn't so bad, I thought. Not a wimp like that bloke she'd brought back from the Operatic. It was just that he wasn't Steve.

There wasn't anyone like my dad.

But she had to have a sex life, I could see that. And it was nice to have a Mum who was fanciable. I felt quite proud of her really – she was looking so sweet in that flowery dress.

"Why is your friend Gilles so gone on Gilles de What's-it?" asked Amy.

"Well Gilles – our Gilles – collects songs and stories from old people," said Angus. "And he reads manuscripts in libraries – the history of Brittany, that sort of thing." I watched the blob of strawberry glaze at the corner of his mouth. "Gilles de Rais was into alchemy in a big way."

"What's alchemy?"

"A kind of magic. They were trying to change ordinary metals into gold."

"That what Gilles wants to do?"

"Well, he's always broke," Angus laughed. "But alchemy's mixed up with ancient Egypt and all sorts of other things. I can see why he's fascinated."

"What other wicked things did Gilles do?" asked Hannah.

"Which Gilles?" teased Angus.

"Oh, you know."

Angus glanced at Martine. "He killed children," he said cautiously. "Hundreds of them."

"Oh, yuk!" said Hannah. She looked warily up at the keep. "In there?"

"Could be."

"Can we go and look?"

"Aren't you scared?"

"Course not." She went over to Angus and took his hand. "Well a bit."

"Does it work?" asked Mum. "This alchemy."

"You thinking of trying it?"

Mum sighed. "Would be nice to be rich."

That night I heard the wolf again.

I was lying in bed wishing Alain would come back. I'd driven him away, I thought wistfully. I wouldn't say no this time.

Oh, shut up, I said when I heard it, but it called again: "*Oohooo-oo...*"

I got out of bed and pulled back the shutters.

"*Oohooo...*" I was about to mimick, when I saw something spotted running into the shadows.

I recognized those spots.

Amy, I thought.

Oh, my God, Amy. She was going to swim in that lake and the wolf was out there.

It was then that I saw Angus...

CHAPTER SIXTEEN

I relit the night-light in its little crimson pot and lay awake for hours trying to sort out my feelings. If Amy and Angus were having it off, why hadn't she told me? We were supposed to be best friends. We told each other everything.

Oh, no we didn't, I reminded myself. Not any more. Love isolated people, made them secretive. Look at me with Alain...

And perhaps I'd misinterpreted. They might have been owl watching. Maybe Angus had a secret passion for astronomy. Maybe they'd been trying to coax out the wolf.

I drifted into a confusion of dreams in which wolf noises became the language of lovers, signals – "*Oohoo*... I'm here... Where are you?" I could hear Amy teasing: "So you look amazing; so what?" Even ancient Henriette was in there somewhere, wrinkled, toothless, yet strangely beautiful, taunting me with her secrets, blinding me with a silken scarf and turning me once, twice, three times. . .

"Oh, tell me, please tell me," I was pleading as I woke up, but even as I drew back the shutters and let in the light, I could still hear Amy's dream voice, infantile, mocking: "We've got a secret and we're not saying."

But *I'm* the chosen one, I thought. It was me Alain called.

Forcing myself back into the real world, I dressed, washed my face and went downstairs. Amy was in the hall playing ping-pong with Hannah, while Angus kept score in a notebook. He looked up at me and grinned.

"Your sister's getting much too good."

I said, "Great."

"Something wrong?" I heard Amy asking as I turned and walked into the kitchen.

Mum was still in her dressing gown. "Hello, love," she said. "Sleep well?"

Martine poured me a coffee without looking up. She was working on a shopping list. "Coke or Vino?" she sang out.

"Beer," called Angus.

"And grenadine," added Hannah.

"What a mixture," said Mum, spreading Mme Auguste's plum jam on a round of baguette.

Martine nibbled the end of her pencil. "We must plan things carefully now," she said. "When we leave on Saturday I don't want to have to throw away half a fridge full."

My heart missed a beat. Leaving? Well, of course we were. This was only a holiday. I looked at the row of copper pots and the scrubbed wooden table always covered with our stuff – drooping posies of wild flowers in jam pots, Amy's dog-eared copy of *Stage*, Hannah's recorder, Mum's fag ends in a saucer and M. Auguste's daily offerings (he'd crept in and out secretly, like a gouty fairy, leaving us lettuces studded with baby slugs, bouquets of carrots and pots of Madame's home-made jam).

I thought of my room upstairs with its fans and its flowers, the hills and hollows of that billowing bed and Alain's dear, familiar face (could I sneak out a snap from that album?). Only three days...

Nothing lasts, I thought sadly. Nothing ever lasts.

"You could surely give any leftovers to the Augustes," Mum was saying.

Martine shook her head. "That would offend their rules of etiquette."

"How silly," I said. How silly, how silly. It had been that kind of fussiness which had kept Alain out of the churchyard.

I watched Martine working at her list. It would have been nice to have talked to her again – in a curious way I felt we shared him – but I could hardly ever find her alone.

Mum picked up my unease. "Nice holiday, love?" she asked unnecessarily, her smile pleading for some kind of approval.

"Oh, fantastic," I said automatically.

"Not over yet." Her attention shifted back to Martine. "So how shall we arrange things?"

Martine considered.

"Why don't we do our shopping late this

afternoon? That would give us the rest of the day free." She glanced up at Amy who'd just come in. "What would you two like to do?"

Outside in the hall I could hear the hollow tick-tock of ping-pong and Hannah's triumphant: "Gotcher!"

Amy said, "Why don't we do one of those walks you're always telling us about?" She looked at me. "What do you think, Ellie?"

"I'm easy," I said coolly.

I remember that day, the day before the barbecue, for the constant ringing of the telephone: Oh, Paul is coming with his girlfriend... *C'était Monique*... Lisa... Gérard... Edouard's sister can't make it... Marie-Luce is coming... That was Guy. He'll be there...

And I remember our sweaty tribal walk under a yellow-grey sky, the jungly smells of warm hedges and flower nectar, the damp of the grass seeping into my worn-out trainers and Angus shaking his fist at the clouds. "Listen God: if it rains tomorrow, I'm suing!"

There was the usual bickering between him and Amy. I understood that now. The arguments, the quarrels, were just another kind of intimacy. Those two had fancied each other from the start.

And the growing tension between Amy and me was neatly overlaid by the presence of Jules trailing rabbits through ditches and hedges, by Hannah fooling about and Martine teaching us dodgy French camping songs which we bawled out inaccurately as we marched along.

"This is one of the ancient roads of France," she told us, "though you'd never guess it now."

We passed an old man with a cartful of hay pulled by two sleepy horses. "*Bonjour*," we murmured dutifully. "*Bonjour . . .*"

Amy paused to watch a couple of butterflies flirting and fluttering: "Look. Butterflies do it in mid-air."

"Oh, Amy," sighed Mum.

Then Jules chased a rabbit into a field of heifers and Martine went berserk. "Jules!" she yelled. "*Viens!*"

"Idiot dog!" shouted Angus. "*Viens ici!*"

After all that, the supermarket should have been a rest cure, but it was there that we had our big row.

Amy nudged me. "Come on – they don't need us."

I followed her.

"Got something to tell you."

"I know."

She looked puzzled. "How could you?"

"I'm psychic," I said acidly.

"Go on, then. Tell me."

That wasn't so easy. It was going to sound as if I'd been spying on them, like some gossipy old cow peering through lace curtains. "Pass," I said.

"I've shown it to Angus," said Amy. Shown what to Angus? I questioned silently. "The inscription on that stone. I thought one of them ought to be told."

I turned ice cold and it wasn't the air conditioning. "You might have asked me."

"Why? I found it, didn't I?" She giggled. "We

175

rowed over to the island last night, when you were all asleep."

"I wasn't asleep."

Amy's hand went to her mouth. "Oh, my God. You saw us?"

"Heard you," I said. "Making those stupid wolf noises."

Amy suddenly caught on. "Is that what's wrong with you?"

"There's nothing wrong with me."

"You fancy him! You're jealous."

"I do not fancy Angus," I was almost weeping, "I have never fancied Angus and I am not jealous," and I turned my back on her and stormed off.

On the ride home we ignored each other, staring stonily out of windows. Mum, caught between us, was baffled. "What's the matter with you two?"

"Nothing," we murmured. "Nothing."

That evening I shared the cooking with Hannah.

"We're all really bad-tempered again, aren't we?" she observed cheerfully.

I brushed chicken legs with oil and turned up the grill. "No, we're not."

"Well, you are."

"Shall we do a big fruit salad?" I said to distract her.

In bed I heard the wolf again, but I didn't respond. The great lovers might have been out there, teasing me, taunting me . . .

The next day dawned blue and perfect. Angus nodded smugly. "God heard. He fixed it. He wouldn't dare disobey me."

"He?" questioned Amy. "Why not She?"

"Don't be stupid," protested Hannah. "You can't have a lady God."

"Why ever not?" snapped Amy.

Martine took the hamburgers out of the freezer. Then she handed Angus a pencilled bill. "Your share of the kitty, *mon fils*."

"OK, OK."

The phone rang and was answered. Then it rang again. I began to wonder if I could fake another headache.

Only two more days now, I thought sadly. I would have preferred to have spent them quietly with the house, communing with its fleeting spirits, sitting in the shade of the bush den listening for the voices of ghosts, waiting for the young Henriette in her white dress to come fluttering up the path, and imagining the soft falling of tennis balls in that phantom court lost among the artichokes and leeks.

That afternoon we took a trip to Noirmoutier, drove across the narrow causeway to the monks' island, ate pancakes in one of the small restaurants and left just before the encroaching tide.

"You're very quiet, Ellie," remarked Mum.

"I'm just tired," I said.

When we got back we found Guy stretched out on the lawn.

He waved. "Contributions in the car." Then he got up. "*Bonne soirée*," he said, kissing Mum and Martine. "And who will be *le cuisinier*?"

"Me, probably," grumbled Angus.

I considered Guy critically, the grey-furred legs

below blue denim shorts, the checked cotton shirt that revealed the beginnings of a paunch, his square, slightly jowly face with its sudden impish smile and the faint pong of the aftershave I still disliked.

And instantly my mind dragged up a flattering still of my dad – the photo Penny from publicity had done when she still had the job. Steve was greyish too, but he was much better looking.

Then I drew in my breath. Steve, I thought. Alain...

Did I have to fancy someone a bit like a young version of my dad?

"I need a galley slave," said Angus. "For the hamburgers."

Sick, I thought. I'm sick. "Do you mind if I drop out?" I said. "I've got a headache." And I wasn't faking it.

"Oh, Ellie, again?" said Mum. "When we get home, I'd better have you looked at."

"I'll be your galley slave," offered Hannah.

Angus looked dubious. "Chopping onions?"

"I can chop onions."

"Shall I be assistant galley slave," offered Martine discreetly.

Amy slipped an arm round my shoulders. "You'll be all right, Ellie. Come on, let's find you some aspirins." We moved into the cool shadows of the house. "I've got some," she said. "Upstairs."

We filled a glass with water and went up to her room. I gulped down two pills, then burst into tears.

"What's wrong, Ellie? What's the matter?"

I sobbed. "Everything."

"You got a period?"

I sniffled and shook my head.

Amy sat down next to me. "We fell out," she said slowly. "That's what's wrong, isn't it? And it was all my fault – I knew you had a thing about that guy. I should never have shown the inscription to Angus. Not without telling you. It was insensitive of me." She looked at me. "Sorry, Ellie."

"Angus is your business," I said shortly. "And if you chose to tell him, that's OK with me."

"It isn't like that," said Amy. "Honest."

I blew my nose. "Sorry." I didn't know what to believe.

But I had to ask her. "What did he say? Did he know about it?"

"Hard to tell. Don't think so, but he might have been faking it." She began stroking my hair. "D'you feel better?"

I nodded.

"Don't drop out, Ellie. It wouldn't be the same without you. And it'll be a great party – a sort of farewell to France." She paused and looked at me. "You *have* got a thing about him, haven't you?"

"No, I haven't," I protested. "I just felt left out. You might have told me."

"I meant the guy in the photograph."

"Oh, Alain?" I said lightly. "Don't be stupid. He's dead."

Amy got up. "Listen. I ought to go down and help. Why don't you just relax, read a book or something? We'll give you a call."

"Oh, thanks," I said gratefully. I needed that island of solitude.

"You should sort out your face." She peered at me. "You've got smudges."

I rubbed the backs of my hands over my sticky cheeks.

"Thanks."

She left, then popped her head back round the door. "What are you going to wear?"

Wear? To a barbecue? I hadn't given it a thought. I glanced down at my jeans. "What I'm wearing now I should think..."

"Well, put your swimsuit on underneath. Then you can swim. Unless you want to go skinny-dipping."

After she left, I went back to my own room. Alain welcomed me home with his sad, shadowy smile. I sat in a bed hollow and stared up at him coldly. Mum hadn't noticed he looked like Steve. "So that's Martine's great-uncle," she'd said once, peering at him through her reading glasses. "The one who died young – yes, he does look romantic."

I studied the portrait. The mouth was wrong; the resemblance was all in the eyes and the shape of the head. Some similarity in the expression though; what was it Martine had said? He's seductive, isn't he?

Well, so was Steve, I assumed. At least Penny thought so.

Was it really my dad I'd fancied in Alain? The idea didn't seem quite so upsetting now. Hadn't I read somewhere that girls were supposed to fancy their dads and boys their mums? It was normal; didn't mean anything lewd.

So I curled up and thought about Amy instead, about her role-playing and the way she was obsessed with make-up and clothes. What are you wearing? she'd asked and it really seemed to matter. I closed my eyes wearily. We hadn't brought that much; there hadn't been space.

Someone put on a tape. It must have been Angus – only Angus would listen to that sort of thing. I found myself wishing he'd turn up the sound – it could grow on you, that old-fashioned jazz. So what would Amy wear? I wondered dreamily. And the two French girls – what was it French women were supposed to have? Chic. I grinned. I could put on that dress. That would shock them. I imagined their voices: "Oh, Ellie. . ."

And the echo came: "Oh, Ettie. . ."

But I'd have to do the thing properly: first things first. The foundation: the bust bodice, my little stockinette girdle. . .

Slowly, sensuously, I rolled the silk stockings over the dark fuzz on my pale winter legs, fastened the tops with suspenders that slid under my tea-rose camiknickers: "Oh, Ettie. . ." He was watching me secretly, my chaperone, my admirer. It was he who lifted my first cocktail dress over my head: "Oh, Ettie. . . Oh, Ettie. . ."

CHAPTER
SEVENTEEN

"Ellie!"

I shook myself awake.

Mum was smiling down at me. "Feeling better, love?"

I nodded dumbly. That dream had disturbed me.

"Get yourself together, then. We're leaving."

Remembering Amy's suggestion, I undressed and put on my swimsuit, drawing over it my Indian skirt with the little fringes so that the swimsuit top looked like a bodice. A bust bodice? I thought. Whatever was that?

I splashed water on my face, and made up, touching my eyelids with greeny-grey shadow and smudging on lipstick.

Downstairs Guy looked me over appreciatively. "You should have worn that dress," he joked. "*Formidable!*"

"I did consider it," I said lightly.

"Oh, Ellie!" laughed Martine; "That dress will

probably end up in some museum when *Tatie* goes."

Amy was wearing gold hoop earrings, and a big silky top over black jeans. She spread a wing of my skirt. "You look great," she said admiringly.

I felt suddenly warmed by that ancient friendship, by the way it could almost die, then resurrect as something new.

Martine was showing off the food. "*Voilà!* All done while you were asleep."

The table was loaded. They'd filled the cold box with sausages and hamburgers and packed cool bags with bottles and cans. Hannah eased out one bottle, showing it off. "*Sirop de grenadine*," she purred.

"We should have bought you some before," said Martine.

"And the barbecue?" asked Guy. "We are not eating raw meat?"

"Oh, that. Courtesy of Edouard's lot."

"What organization!" exclaimed Guy.

"I'm riding in Gee's car," announced Hannah. "But in the front this time."

"Don't you want to go with your friend Cathérine?"

Hannah pulled a face. "Her? She's just a kid."

Guy looked pleased. "I would be honoured, *mademoiselle*," he said solemnly, and Hannah went all soppy. "And your mother and sister in the back?"

That left Amy with Angus. Fine by me, I thought. It would be a change to have Mum to myself.

Outside the lodge Catherine and Marie-Luce

183

were waiting in the Peugeot. We slowed down to greet them, Hannah waving regally from the front seat: "*Salut! Bonsoir!*" The Augustes stood, smiling at the three car convoy. "*Au revoir! Au revoir!*"

We moved along the main road, and then, in a pre-sunset haze, turned west towards St Brévin and the sea.

I can still smell the warm pines, and the fragrance of all the suppers being cooked in those bleached summer shanties. I can still see the drifts of sand blurring the edges of the road, and the dark bush of Amy's hair next to Angus's tawny head through the back window of the Volvo. Inside our car Hannah was playing her recorder, going through her repertoire to impress Guy, and on the back seat I had Mum all to myself and found I had nothing to say.

Martine spotted Edouard's van and she slowed, flagging us all down. We parked and unloaded, trudging with our burdens through the narrow fringe of pines and on to the beach. The tide was way out, the sea a shifting expanse of rose-flecked silvers, and trails of tadpole-black seaweed streaked the flat, newly-exposed sand.

The two kids ran ahead, Hannah's tasselled recorder bag (a creation of Mum's) bouncing away on her back. We followed them more soberly, Angus with Amy and Marie-Luce, Martine with Guy, and tongue-tied me with Mum.

At the edge of the dunes we could see people setting up a barbecue. I picked out Edouard, then Gilles.

There was a brief burst of flame.

"That's it," said Martine. "They've got it going."

Gilles looked up. "*Salut!*" He popped open a bottle: "*Olé!*" and poured it foaming and bubbling into paper cups.

"*Mais c'est du Champagne*," murmured Guy. "*On est très snob, ce soir.*"

"One is loaded," murmured Martine suspiciously.

"Can I have some?" said Hannah.

"Just this once," said Mum.

A couple of stray dogs came sniffing round the boxes. "Keep them covered!" yelled Martine.

More people arrived with packets and bottles, with salads in plastic bowls, round quiches in silver-foil cases, cheeses and crinkly crisps. *Salut, salut*... Kiss, kiss..."

The sun, pulled by the sea, swelled and flushed crimson. "What a sky!" said Amy. "What a sunset! Wow!"

Angus put on Martine's blue-and-white striped apron and brought out the chef's paper hat he'd picked up in Pornic.

"*Pas encore*," scolded Martine. "You have to wait until the charcoal is ready."

Someone set up a couple of camping tables with adjustable feet, burying the legs in the sand. Soon their plastic tops were covered with bottles and bowls.

Angus held up a tumbler: "Grenadine for someone!" and Hannah squealed, "Me! Me!"

Edouard topped up my drink. "*Ça va?*"

I nodded.

Behind us, a crocodile of kids led by a couple

of girls plodded two by two towards the road. Gilles licked his lips and pointed. "A feast for Barbe Bleue."

"Ooh, you're nasty," said Hannah.

"*Une colonie de vacances*," said Martine dreamily.

"What's that?" asked Amy.

"Oh, you know – I've told you already. A children's camp. There are lots round here. Most French children go on one. I used to."

"Bet you gave your *moniteurs* a hard time," teased Angus.

Martine chuckled. "I think I probably did."

Someone put on a tape – a weird French rock band they all seemed to find funny. A few of them started fooling about, disco dancing. Amy's earrings winked a rosy copper as she moved, her round bum swinging like a pendulum inside that big splashy top.

Angus began loading the barbecue, helped by a bloke I'd never seen, somebody's brother, cousin, boyfriend. I grabbed a handful of crisps and wandered off with my freshly brimming cup. I didn't much like parties, but this one was different. In the distance I could see the smoke of another barbecue – the huddle of people and the thin lilac haze hanging in the tangerine air. It felt warm, primitive. We were like little tribes, I thought happily, on a desert island.

I returned with my cup empty, but it was instantly refilled. There was a fairy tale, I remembered vaguely, with a goblet that did that.

Mum came up to me, her cheeks peached from

sunset and her eyes all shiny. "Go easy on the booze, Ellie."

I was livid. "I am nearly sixteen, in case you've forgotten. Don't tell me how to behave!" It was the first thing I'd said to her since we'd left the house.

Defeated, she melted back into the crowd and I drifted, my head light and full of champagne bubbles. I saw dancing bodies stained by the dying sun, hair tinged strawberry, lips maroon. And all around me flowed the swift patter of French, fast, tough and incomprehensible. It was like falling headlong into a foreign film with no subtitles and I floated, I drowned in its alien sounds.

Someone came up to me. "*Anglaise?*"

I nodded smugly. For once I didn't have to dream up clever things to say. I was English. I was foreign.

"The English are beautiful," he said, and he began to dance, moving his body with the rhythm of the band, and I, who never danced, never made a fool of myself, looked into that stranger's face, smiled, flirted, and began to move, swing, felt my body respond to the insistent beat-beat, my skirt rising and and swaying like the petals of a flower, like the crinkly petals of the petunias in Mum's window box.

Angus yelled, "*On mange!* We eat!"

And straight away I exchanged my sexy stranger for a hamburger and three sizzling sausages. I didn't need sexy strangers. I was Alain's girl. I'd never bothered with others at the tea dances at Nantes; why should this be any different?

Hannah came looking for me. "Ooh, Ellie, I saw

you. I didn't know you could dance."

I blinked. "You don't know everything about me," I hinted mysteriously, and I grabbed up her hands and we pranced about.

Out of the corner of my eye I noticed that Sexpot Amy had hogged Gilles again, sitting close up to him, sharing his sandpit. Gaëlle and another girl were in there too, with a few blokes I hadn't met. I looked round for Annick and saw her isolated, puffing on a cigarette.

I dropped Hannah's hands and went over to her. "*Salut.*"

She picked up my sympathy. "He is always like that."

"Why do you put up with it?"

She fingered the little silver rings in her earlobe. "He is – *artiste*," she said reverently. "Much talent. *Je l'admire.*" She dropped her stub and toed sand over it. "Men flirt," she said. "*C'est rien.*" Then she smiled her wide, glittery smile. "We join them, yes?'

"OK," I said.

Gilles was playing again, almost privately, concentrating, the soft, unamplified melody half smothered by the sound of the tape. We sat close to him, straining to hear, Annick leaning now against his thigh, Amy pressed against his side.

He looked up and his dark eyes held me. "Good party, English?"

I nodded.

From somewhere, Martine's voice began trilling, "*I know a youth who loves a little maid. . .*" and they turned down the tape to encourage her.

Gilles suddenly stopped playing. "The girl who ran away," he said.

I was puzzled. "Who is?"

He grinned and pointed at me.

"But I didn't..."

"The Ouija board?"

In the violet dusk my flush went unnoticed. "I was tired," I said carefully.

"You were scared, you mean," said Amy. Her voice lowered with awe. "You were called."

Gaëlle and some of the others had moved back to the barbecue. Amy got up too. "I'm going for a refill," she said. "Can I fetch you anything?"

"Not you, Ellie," Gilles was saying. "You were not called."

My mouth felt stiff. "No," I said to Amy. "Thanks." Not me? Not Ellie?

I heard a male voice, *"Hey, but I think that little maid will die..."* and saw Guy with his arms round Martine and Mum, the three of them prancing ridiculously, bobbing up and down, their faces pink and shiny with sweat.

"Not me?" I repeated dumbly. "Not me?"

Gilles popped open a can of beer and stood it in the sand between my feet.

"Not Ellie," he explained. "Ettie." He smiled. "They all know, the old ones. My own *grand-mère* – she know."

Annick became visibly upset. *"Oh non, Gilles. Il ne faut pas dire."*

"Pourquoi pas? Ellie was frightened so I tell her." He slipped his arm round Annick, but leaned over towards me. "The Ouija is old," he said. "The letters

are . . ." He struggled for the word.

Once again I felt that jigsaw piece falling into place.

"The two 'L's . . ."

The pattern was complete but I couldn't bear to look.

"They were 'T's." He pronounced the letter: "Tay". "You understand now?" He looked pleased with himself. "Angus was there so we could not tell you."

I retreated behind confusion. "Tell me what?" I said, posing the question for which I did not want an answer.

Gilles shook his head in disbelief. Then he put out his hand and cupped my chin. "That you are sexy, English." His breath smelt of wine and spices and my mouth went all soft for the kiss that never came. "Alain loved his sister," he spelled out. "When she became – " and he cupped his hands graphically over his stomach – "he kill himself."

Annick struggled to her feet. "*Pas nécessaire*," she snapped.

Rigid with shock, I watched her striding away, her blonde hair electric and her bare feet kicking up angry sprays of sand. Then I turned back to Gilles.

"And her baby?" I asked weakly.

"Not allowed." He shrugged. "*C'était la bour-geoisie*." He pulled me closer, but I moved away. "You English," he complained. "So cold . . ."

Hannah came wriggling out of the crowd, dragging Cathérine by the hand. "Angus said you did magic," she said. The two of them slithered into the sandpit. "Show us."

"Magic?" Gilles pantomimed surprise. "Me?"

"Yes, you can. Ellie knows, don't you, Ellie? Show us."

Gilles reached for his guitar. "Music is magic."

"Don't be stupid," said Hannah and she took out her recorder and blew him a blast. "Anyone can do music."

Gilles snatched it out of her hands. "*Pas gentil*," he reprimanded. The tune he picked out sounded high and ghostly, a medieval dance of love. Or death.

Hannah started wriggling. "Show us some magic," she pleaded. "Please. I've never seen any real magic."

"...*de la magie, monsieur*," squeaked Cathérine.

Gilles packed away his guitar, slinging it over one shoulder. "OK." He stood up, still holding Hannah's recorder. "But not here. You come. You follow me..." He looked at me invitingly, but I shook my head.

I sat, watching their silhouettes blur, hearing that high, haunting jig fade into nothing as the Pied Piper and his children went dancing into the night. Then I got up and went off in search of a drink or another sexy stranger, I didn't care which.

For I had known all the time...

I had known that night I'd been called from the garden: "Ettie, Ettie", heard the unmistakable rasp of the "T" in the middle, thought Amy was fooling.

And like a puppet on strings I wandered, I

flirted, I danced and I smiled, and all the time I kept thinking: it wasn't me he wanted.

My name was Ellie. Ellie.

"Ellie, you all right?" It was Martine, fussing.

"Course I am," I said thickly.

"Have you seen Cathérine? Marie-Luce wants to leave."

"She's with Hannah."

Mum appeared from nowhere, hanging on to Guy's hand. "So where's Hannah?" she asked.

Hannah, Hannah, I thought. What about Ellie? What about me? "How would I know?" I narked.

"You might keep an eye on her."

"So might you," I said bitchily.

Martine stepped in briskly. "They are probably not far." She raised her voice. "Hannah? Cathérine?"

Suddenly I remembered. "They've gone off with Gilles."

"With Gilles?" screeched Martine. "And you let them?"

"So what's wrong with Gilles?"

"Nothing," said Angus who had just joined in. "My mother's prejudices, that's all. He's got long hair, he makes the wrong kind of music, that's enough for her." He turned to me. "Come on; we'll dig them out. Which way did they go?"

I showed him, then followed him blindly. Hannah, I thought, but my head was spinning.

Little Hannah, I thought, and my feet thumped out a horrid rhythm in the sand: Bluebeard, Bluebeard, Bluebeard. . .

Amy went swanning past us in a swimsuit, her

hair flying. "Come on, Ellie! Come on, Angus! It's not cold."

"Seen Hannah?" called Angus.

"Seen Gilles?" I asked. De Rais, I added silently. Bluebeard. I'd read his story in that castle. First he screwed them. Then he tortured them.

Amy hesitated. "No."

"Hannah's gone missing," said Angus. "With Cathérine."

"And Gilles," I insisted. And then he killed them.

Killed. Killed.

"They'll be OK," said Amy, "if they're with Gilles."

"That was some time ago," said Angus. "They may not be now."

Amy looked alarmed. "I'll help you search."

"Try up there, then." Angus pointed to the dark fringe of pines. "We'll do the beach."

We caught up with someone else's party. "Cathérine!" we yelled. "Hannah!"

"*Deux fillettes*," gasped Angus. "*Vous avez vu?*"

Blank faces. "*Mais non... Mais non...*"

I stopped. "Angus, look." Towards the sea, on the sand flats, I'd spotted a dark huddle and a figure prodding at the ground.

"Fishermen," said Angus. "Digging for worms."

We ran down to check and found Cathérine and Hannah squatting inside a five-sided shape drawn on the damp sand.

"Come on," we shouted. "They're all out looking for you."

Hannah glared at me.

"Go away," she said. "This is private."

I looked at the long creamy frills of the growing waves, watched the water clawing at the land. "Tide's turning," I said. "You'll get soaked."

"We're not allowed to come out of our magic house," Hannah pointed at the sand drawing, "or the demons will get us."

Gilles came stepping out of the shadows, making us jump.

"*Tu es idiot!*" shouted Angus. "What do you think you're doing?"

"*De la magie*," said Gilles. "A pentagram – so." He offered us a pull of the joint he was smoking. "For you too." He pointed out to sea. "You watch," he said. He seemed to be in some kind of a trance. "We make Montoise rise . . ."

Angus grabbed the joint and hurled it away. "Listen," he said. "These kids have to get back."

Catherine smoothed down her dress and looked smug.

Hannah glowered. "Go away," she said. "You're spoiling everything."

Gilles took out his guitar and began to sing, some chanty folksong in a language I supposed to be Breton.

Hannah yawned. "I don't see what this has to do with magic."

"You watch," said Gilles. He turned to Angus. "That was good stuff," he complained, "and you waste it." He muttered some words; then he half closed his eyes. "Listen. I hear the church bells under the water." He cupped his hand round

Hannah's small ear, then Cathérine's. "You hear them?"

Hannah nodded slowly, her face suddenly rapt.

"And now we see the roofs and the..." His English was failing him, but he kept up the spell. "The roofs..."

"And the lights in the windows," squealed Hannah. "Oh, yes I can see."

Cathérine pointed, her eyes shining. "*Regarde*," she whispered.

"It's only a ship," said Angus.

"No, it's not," said Hannah.

Angus made a grab for Cathérine, but she fought and kicked. "*On y va*," he insisted helplessly, trying to hold her down.

"I'm going in," announced Hannah, wriggling out of her shorts and top. "I'm going to swim out to that town."

"No, you're not!" I made a grab for her, but missed.

All at once Gilles looked concerned. "She can swim?"

"Why would you care?" I shrieked. I ran after her, but there were others drawn by the incoming tide – a kid who could have been Hannah but wasn't, a mongrel running splash-splash through the first glistening shallows and people from the party, shrieking and jumping the waves.

"Hannah!" I called out. "Hannah!" I dropped my skirt on the beach and waded in. "Hannah."

Then suddenly I saw what she must have seen – in the middle distance, rising, a huddle of houses with torches flickering orange, slated turrets and a tall spire, thatched roofs and stone arches and figures moving.

And there was Alain, beckoning, beckoning...

I fought against the tide. The waves chopped into my face. "Alain!" I called.

And he held out his arms to me: "*Viens, mon amour...*"

The water slapped over my head, but when I came up coughing all the torches of Montoise were dancing in my eyes. Not much further, not much further. I could hear him saying my name.

"Ettie... Ettie..."

My tears mixed with the sea. "But I'm Ellie," I gasped.

I turned away and found Hannah bobbing up and down in the waves. "Oh, it's going," she was wailing. "Oh, it's gone!" And when I looked back there was nothing.

No torches, no houses, no spire. No Alain.

It was over.

"Let's go back," I said harshly and the sea rolled us in.

When we picked up my skirt, half soaked by the tide, Hannah slipped her hand into mine.

"Ellie," she asked. "Was it real?"

I closed my eyes.

"It was just a reflection," I said firmly, "of the lights on that ship."

CHAPTER EIGHTEEN

Morning comes, bringing no further snow. The light is now London November, flat, sunless, white with no radiance. It worries me awake. Or was I awake anyway? I'm not sure whether I was dreaming or just reminiscing. I lift the curtain and peer across at Hannah, still asleep with her feet sticking out. Her holiday souvenirs – the bread sheaves and her beloved straw hat – hang on the wall over her bed. She looks, I think fondly, about five.

I grin. She would not be flattered.

Crawling out, I dress quickly for my Saturday job – tights, skirt and a blouse. I can hear Mum bumbling around, warbling her lines against the running of a tap, so I plug in the kettle and mix her a coffee. By the time she's flushed the loo, it's lukewarm, but she drinks it anyway.

We eat on an island surrounded by taffetas, felts, gold braid and sequins, plus the tottering pile of exercise books she'd stayed up late to mark.

"You've been reading that script again," I tease her.

"It's the first time they've given me a part."

"It's only two lines," I say. "You're not going to muff those. And you have got another couple of weeks."

But she insists. "It's got to be good." She talks thickly, her mouth full of muesli.

"Oh, it will be, Mum. You'll be brilliant. Stop worrying."

"Any post?" she calls out as I open the front door.

I know what she's asking.

Yes, he did write. Twice. A postcard to all three of us from the Cote d'Azur — one of those "Wish You Were Here" jobs. And then a brief note to her. Maybe she'll get a Christmas card.

Guy wasn't so bad. For a holiday romance.

I catch the bus down to the The Last Crumpet. During the week they've done up the windows for Christmas. There's a cake iced like a ski slope, a gingerbread house with fairy lights, chocolate logs with robin redbreasts and stacks of mince pies on pierced silver platters. The obligatory wedding cake (orders taken) has a mistletoe arch over the bridal pair, and there's tinsel all over the place — the old-fashioned spidery kind that really twinkles.

"You're late," Sandra complains.

It's only fifteen minutes.

I mouth "Sorry," but I'm not. I feel light. I feel free.

I'd stopped myself thinking about Chanteloup.

"Nice holiday?" people had asked. "Great," I'd said vaguely, dredging up some stereotyped image of seaside and France.

But the shadow of Alain still hovered, elusive, forbidden. And I found myself looking for his features in strangers, trying to give the ghost flesh; exorcise it.

Even now. Even yesterday.

I smile. Old habits are hard to drop.

I put on my frilly apron, pin that silly pink band over my hygienically tied-back hair, and my heart soars. Behind me the loaves multiply in the arched mirrors garlanded with fake holly. Things just fell into place, I think happily. It was all there, but I just couldn't see.

A queue has been forming on the other side of the glass counter.

I switch on my patter. "A round rye? A wholemeal? Thank you madam. Yes, we do bake on the premises. Two dozen mince pies? I'll get you a box. Pizza? Shall I put it in the microwave? And two slices of apple tart..."

Someone says, "You ought to cover it all up."

I blink and I'm looking at Amy.

"Think of us slimmers," she moans. She takes a deep breath. "This lot's strictly for my family: two Eccles cakes, six mince pies and a strawberry flan." She grins. "And make it snappy, slave."

"Yes, madam," I say humbly.

She watches me make up two boxes. "Aren't you a pro?"

"I ought to be," I say. "I had enough practice in the summer."

Her face goes all funny. She's up to something; I know she is. "I got in," she says smugly.

I curl the ribbons with a knife and stand the boxes on the counter. "Got in where?"

"The Poly panto, dope. Yesterday." She hands me a fiver. "Said I'd do anything to get on the stage and they took me at my word. But I need an assistant so I signed you on too."

"You cow!"

For some unknown reason this sets her off.

"It's a great part," she snorts. "No lines to learn."

I drop the change into her outstretched palm. "I told you already. No!"

She leans towards me. "Back end or front end?"

I'm suitably intrigued. "Of what?"

Amy looks triumphant. "Daisy. The cow."

"Oh no," I shriek.

"Why not? We could be unforgettable."

I think of her latest boyfriend. "Ask Martin," I joke.

"Oh, you'd be much better," she tells me. "You've got talent."

For what? I ask myself. "See you tonight," I say firmly. Be more positive, I think, or she'll talk you into it. "Amy!" I yell after her. "I'm not doing it!"

"OK, OK."

"If you'd stop chattering to your friends," complains a sharp-edged woman in a flashy parka, "maybe some of us could get served."

Old bat, I think.

Sandra frowns as if she's psychic, and I am instantly contrite. "Sorry, madam," I say humbly.

With Christmas so close, I can't afford to lose my job.

Outside the window I can see Amy lifting the side of the box, can almost hear her drool.

"Ellie, wake up!" snaps Sandra.

I put on one of my freshly-thawed smiles.

"Can I help you, madam?" Incest ("That'll be three pounds exactly") can happen in the nicest families.

I'd been a rat, I realize three months too late. To Martine and she'd only been trying to protect me.

Poor Martine, is she sad? She was really fond of old Henriette. I suddenly want to do something nice to make up, but I can't think what.

On the stroke of one thirty, Tim and Maggie arrive, punctual as usual.

"All change," says Maggie, her face dark and sculptural, her hair shorn to a gelled quiff. "Busy morning?"

In the back room I hang up my hat and my apron. I am putting on my anorak when Sandra breezes in.

"End of the month, Ellie," she says, handing me a sealed envelope. "December's going to be frantic. Try to keep your mind on your job, dear – I can easily replace you, but I'd rather not."

I pick up three Cornish pasties for our lunch, not opening the envelope until I'm safely on the bus. Only then do I take a peek. Fifty quid. I'm loaded! Straight away I start to budget. Ten quid for Mum, proper earrings to replace my studs, the rest towards Christmas presents. Maybe something for Martine – Belgian chocolates, a plant in a pot – but I have to talk to her. I haven't seen her alone since we came back from Chanteloup.

Mum puts the pasties in the microwave.

"No chocolate fudge cake?" grumbles Hannah.

I suddenly have this crazy idea. Doesn't Martine do a Saturday surgery?

Mum is stirring butter into the peas. I ask her obliquely, "You seeing Martine this afternoon?"

She dumps the plates on the table. "Martine's working. You know that."

"You helping her with the party?"

"It isn't her party, is it? She passed *her* driving test twenty-five years ago." Then she relents. "Later, maybe. Then Angus will have to take over, because we've got a rehearsal."

I'm casual. "OK if I make a phone call?"

She trots out her usual un-joky joke: "As long as it isn't New York."

I close the door so I can't be heard.

"Can I make an appointment to see Mrs Hamilton? This afternoon? You've got a cancellation? That's fantastic. The name? Oh." I have to think quickly; I want to take her by surprise. "Susan," I say. "Susan Brown."

I am already beginning to feel a fool when I walk into the waiting room in Harrington Road, with my bunch of chrysanthemums in crackly cellophane printed all over with: SAY IT WITH FLOWERS.

The receptionist looks up and smiles.

"Aren't they lovely?" she says. "Name?"

"Ellie – " I correct myself quickly. "Susan Brown," I say boldly. "I rang earlier."

"Oh yes, the cancellation. Take a seat please, Miss Brown."

I'm not sure what to do with my bouquet – I feel like a bridesmaid holding it on my lap. I try balancing it across a cushion, but it falls on its head. Finally I prop it upright in the corner of an armchair, and hide behind one of those glossy monthlies only dentists seem to buy.

At twenty past three a young woman with a toddler comes out of the surgery. "Bye, Mrs Hamilton."

I wait nervously. It isn't too late to make a run for it. I could give the flowers to Mum. Martine would never know. She's expecting Susan Brown, isn't she?

But the receptionist nails me.

"Mrs Hamilton will see you now." She watches me struggling with the flowers. "Do you want to leave those with me? You can pick them up on your way out."

"That's all right," I mutter foolishly.

Martine has her back turned. She's washing her hands.

I say, "Martine," and she whips round. "Ellie. What are you doing here?"

I hold out the flowers. My arm feels stiff and about a mile long. "For you," I say stupidly.

She takes them. "Thank you, Ellie. But why?"

"I wanted to say how sorry I was about . . ." I stall. "Henriette . . ."

"Chrissie told you then."

203

"Yesterday, yes."

She looks about for a suitable container, then stands the flowers in the sink, half filling it with water.

"Yours is my last appointment, so I'll take them straight home with me." She hugs me and I am enveloped in her perfume. "You are a sweet girl," she tells me, and she gives me two kisses as usual, one on each cheek. "Sit down." She waves at the dental chair. "It's all we've got, I'm afraid." She opens the door. "Could you do us two coffees, Tricia? Then you can go. This isn't a patient – it's a friend of mine."

Not just the daughter of a friend? I feel oddly flattered.

She takes off her white coat and sits astride the high swivelling stool, her beige skirt stretched between her solid thighs.

"You have come to spy on me, I think." Her eyes twinkle. "To see if I sing opera while I drill teeth?"

I feel guilty: "Oh, no!" I eye Martine affectionately over a glassful of pink mouthwash – her voluminous, grey-flecked auburn hair, her wide hips and the soft mounds of her breasts under her black wrapover shirt.

Suddenly it's easy. "I really came to say sorry."

She shrugs. "Henriette was very old. It was to be expected."

"Not just about Henriette... I was a bit of a pain at Chanteloup."

"Oh, Ellie, that was months ago. And you were

under stress." She changes the subject. "The funeral's on Tuesday. We shall cross tomorrow night." Then she treats me to one of her hard looks. "It will be a double funeral," she says and I gasp.

She'd known about that stone all the time!

"A liberal young priest." She shrugs. "There are those in the family who still disapprove. *Que voulez-vous*? They were strict in those days. She was chaperoned constantly. But the only lover he allowed anywhere near her was himself. A possessive man, Alain." She began bustling about, switching things off. "The youngest son . . . a great future they had planned for him."

I remembered my own version of Alain's story. A lawyer? I wondered. An accountant?

"They should have let him paint."

"Alain?" Martine laughed. "Don't you mean Henriette? They sent him to Nantes, but he would not study. Too many women, too much wine. . . After one year he was back home, making trouble again." She looked at me. "It wasn't your fault, Ellie. I think you must have been some kind of focus. As I was once." She touched up her lipstick in the mirror, distorting her mouth. "You know I said Alain was seductive. . ." She turned. "Well, so was she. Remember those snapshots?"

I nod.

"Not all Alain's fault, I think." She smiles at me. "My grandmother told me a little – the rest I picked up from gossip. We were young; they thought we didn't understand. But nobody speaks of it."

"Does Angus know?"

"I could never tell him. Maybe his friends? But you?" She smiles at me warmly. "You are so close to him these days."

"But it's family," I protest. "That wouldn't be right."

"You are wise, Ellie..."

She scoops up her bouquet, swaddling the dripping stems in tissues. "These are lovely."

We leave together.

"You would like a lift?"

"I'll come back and help if you like."

"Oh, that would be good. You cook well."

The Volvo still smells of France, of holiday, of Chanteloup.

Martine turns on the engine. "Things are different now for women," she says. "Look at me. Look at you." We start climbing the hill. "Henriette was talented. She wanted to study in Paris, but they wouldn't let her go. A woman's place is in the home, I think you say here? It must have been..." and she gave a little shudder, "stifling. Alain seduced her, but she encouraged him. She took her revenge on that family. Poor Henriette."

I am silent. I am shocked.

"She got pregnant," I say at last. "But it could have been anybody."

"Not in that family. It must have been blatant — everyone knew the name of the father."

"And the baby?"

She sighs. "They would have known how to deal with a problem like that. All tidy; all hush-hush; no baby. Perhaps they sent her away. For him it must have been the end. It wasn't just sex. Alain was screwed up, but I think he loved her."

I study Martine's profile. He is nothing like her, I think for the hundredth time. Apart from the colouring. And that short, solid nose and those high cheekbones, they come from his dad.

But the shape of Angus's mouth, and those deep-set, soulful eyes?

They come from much further back . . .